Hannah exited the bathroom wrapped in a towel. Now, why was the closet door open? She slammed it shut.

"Hey! What the hell?"

The masculine voice catapulted Hannah into action.

Even in Minnesota she'd heard stories of marauding bandits who robbed hotel rooms and did who-knew-what-else to innocent travelers.

She slammed her shoulder into the closet door and braced her bare feet. This guy wasn't going to abscond with her meager store of cash.

"Get away from the damn door!" the voice bellowed. Masculine. Determined. And very angry.

Not a chance, she vowed. She glanced down at the side of the bed. *Cowboy boots?*

Size twelve, at least, and well-worn like those of a man who was used to riding the range. A tough man. A dangerous man. Shoes told a lot about a person.

Hannah swallowed hard. Why would an intruder put his boots beside *her* bed?

"Let me outta here!"

On the other side of the door the owner of the cowboy boots shoved hard. Hannah locked her knees and held on. No way was she going to give in. Her very life—and possibly her tenacious virginity—might depend upon it.

Lord, why had she bothered to save *that,* only to lose it to some hotel cat burglar?

Dear Reader,

We have two exciting and very different stories for your enjoyment. Gwen Pemberton is a talented new author who won the Golden Heart Award for best short contemporary romance novel at the national 1996 Romance Writers of America conference. At the glamorous awards banquet—the Oscars of the romance world—an excited Gwen accepted her statuette and was able to announce that she had sold that book, her first novel, to Love & Laughter. We hope you will enjoy her winning entry, *Wooing Wanda,* as much as the judges did!

Charlotte Maclay, a favorite with readers of Harlequin American Romance, has written a delightful tale of opposites forced to share a hotel room in a convention-filled Chicago. It's the story of a heroine, a straitlaced lingerie designer, who's just dying to be *bad,* and a hero who's determined to keep his hands off! Fun and games ensue throughout *Accidental Roommates.*

So give yourself an evening off—you deserve it!— curl up with a good book and indulge yourself with Love & Laughter!

Humorously yours,

Malle Vallik

Malle Vallik
Associate Senior Editor

ACCIDENTAL ROOMMATES
Charlotte Maclay

Harlequin Books

TORONTO • NEW YORK • LONDON
AMSTERDAM • PARIS • SYDNEY • HAMBURG
STOCKHOLM • ATHENS • TOKYO • MILAN
MADRID • WARSAW • BUDAPEST • AUCKLAND

ISBN 0-373-44029-4

ACCIDENTAL ROOMMATES

Copyright © 1997 by Charlotte Lobb

A funny thing happened...

As a child, I was convinced there were tiny people inside my television. I'd even try to catch them off guard by changing the station really fast. But I grew up and married an engineer, who patiently explained everything I saw on the television floated to me on the ether. *Right!*

Eventually we bought a computer. And guess what?

All those tiny people are now running around inside my computer having a wonderful time. They lead interesting and intriguing lives, some of which I am able to capture on paper. I'm so glad you'll let me share their stories with you and hope they leave you smiling.

I enjoy hearing from readers: P.O. Box 505, Torrance, CA 90508

—Charlotte Maclay

Books by Charlotte Maclay

HARLEQUIN AMERICAN ROMANCE
537—THE KIDNAPPED BRIDE
585—THE COWBOY & THE BELLY DANCER
620—THE BEWITCHING BACHELOR
643—WANTED: A DAD TO BRAG ABOUT
657—THE LITTLEST ANGEL
684—STEALING SAMANTHA

1

STAYING IN a four-star hotel wasn't *all* that extravagant, Hannah Jansen rationalized, reveling in the texture of the outrageously fluffy towel wrapped around her wet hair. This was business, after all. If the lingerie buyers' convention was going to be held here, this was where she had to be. Assuming she wanted to sell her designs to a major retail outlet.

Which she did. No question.

She stepped out of the shower and wrapped another deliciously plush towel around her body. Now this was the life, she thought, smiling into the fogged mirror that stretched the length of the bathroom. Simulated gold filigree bordered the faux marble bathroom tiles and there was a lovely pedestal sink with gold taps.

If the folks in Crookston, Minnesota could see her now, wouldn't they laugh!

As she pulled open the bathroom door, a puff of steam preceded her into the bedroom. A king-size bed was to her right and a giant walk-in closet to her—

Now how had that door been left open?

She slammed the door shut.

"Hey! What the hell?"

The masculine voice catapulted Hannah into action.

Even in Minnesota she'd heard stories of marauding bandits who robbed hotel rooms in big cities like Chicago and did who knew what else to innocent travelers.

She slammed her shoulder into the closet door and braced her bare feet. This guy wasn't going to abscond with any of her meager store of cash. Or lay a single pinky on her body, she thought trembling slightly at the idea.

"Get away from the damn door!" the voice bellowed. Masculine. Determined. And very angry.

Not a chance, mister, she vowed. Not until she had a whole flotilla of cops to back her up.

She glanced down at the side of the bed.

Cowboy boots?

Size twelve, at least, and well-worn like those of a man who was used to riding the range. A tough man. A dangerous man. Shoes told a lot about a person. The message she was getting about this guy was downright scary.

Hannah swallowed hard. Why would an intruder put his boots beside *her* bed?

She needed to reach the phone on the bedside table so she could call security.

"Let me outta here!"

The owner of the cowboy boots shoved hard on

the other side of the door. Hannah locked her knees and held on. No way was she going to give in. Her very life—and possibly her tenacious virginity—might depend upon it.

Lord, why had she bothered to save *that*, only to lose it to some hotel cat burglar?

When the pressure eased on her shoulder, she lifted one leg, stretching her toes to the maximum, and angled for the phone. She'd almost reached it when—

A large, very male figure burst out of the closet, blasting past her as his weight threw open the door.

The force of his explosive exit from the closet caused her to tumble to the floor. She curled up cowering in the corner between the bed and the wall. "No, don't!" she cried, ashamed of the cowardice that made her scrunch her eyes closed tight and abandon her vow to be courageous. "I don't have much money but it's yours. All of it."

"Why would I want your money?"

She cracked one eye open. The man glaring down at her was *big*. His dark hair and thick eyebrows made him a thoroughly imposing figure. "You're not here to rob me?"

"Mostly, lady, I want to know why the hell you're in my hotel room."

"*Your* room?"

"You've got that damn straight. Now either tell me what the hell is going on, or I'm going to call security."

He was going to call security? *She* was the one who was about to be ravaged. Wasn't she?

She squirmed into a more upright sitting position, taking care that the towel wrapped around her continued to provide some small degree of modesty. Hannah was not used to going toe-to-toe with a broad-shouldered cowboy when she herself was virtually naked. A decidedly disadvantageous position.

"Sir, I assure you, this is *my* room. If you doubt that, you might wish to check the card key on the desk. *My* card key, which gave me access to this room an hour ago."

As Hannah huddled in the corner, the stranger walked across the room. Actually, *swaggered* was a better description of the way he moved even though he was barefoot. He had incredibly lean hips, tight buns, and thighs molded by stonewashed denim that fit like a second skin.

If she hadn't been so frightened, Hannah would have been fascinated by the slim, sexy look of the stranger. And shamed by the unwelcome and startling acceleration of her heartbeat.

As far as she knew, the man could be a serial killer.

She didn't relish the thought of being his next victim, however sexy he was.

He picked up her card key, gave her another threatening look, took two more long-legged strides to the door and yanked it open.

"Would you mind!" she complained as a cold

blast of air swept through the room. "I don't have any clothes on."

"I noticed, lady. Believe me, I noticed."

The heat of a blush started somewhere around her big toe, then sped upward to flame in her cheeks.

Jamming the key in the lock, he waited a moment before the telltale green light flashed on. "I'll be damned," he muttered.

Repeating the process with a key card he pulled from his pocket, he concluded, "Looks like there's been some mistake." He let the door swing shut.

"How clever of you to recognize there's been an error." Feeling somewhat relieved, she struggled up to sit on the edge of the bed. The longer the stranger looked at her, the more the towel that was wrapped precariously around her seemed to shrink to minuscule proportions. His silver-blue eyes were bracketed by attractive squint lines.

"If you'll just get your things," she suggested, "you can go back to the registration desk and straighten out the mistake. No harm done." Only a little aerobic exercise for her heart.

"It was a zoo downstairs when I checked in. The bellboy hasn't sent my things up yet."

"Well, good. You can save him a wasted trip."

One corner of his mouth quirked into a faint smile. "I'm Holt Janson. Pleased to meet you."

"Hannah Jansen," she automatically responded,

not quite so confident that she was pleased with this situation.

"Janson?" he echoed. "With an *o*?"

"With an *e*."

"Ah. I think we've found the cause of our problem."

"*Your* problem. I really wish you'd leave now."

"That may not be possible. I heard the desk clerk telling folks the hotel is all filled up."

"I'm sure they can find another room for you."

"I saw one guy offer a crisp hundred-dollar bill to the clerk, and it didn't do any good."

She certainly didn't have a hundred-dollar bill, crisp or otherwise, to bargain with. "There are other hotels in Chicago."

"All booked. There are mega conventions in town. That's why the guy offered a bribe. He was desperate."

Hannah was beginning to share a similar feeling. "Look, Mr. Jansen—"

"With an *o*."

"Yes, well, I'm hoping you'll be a gentleman about this little mix up we've experienced. I'm sure the front desk will do everything it can to rectify the problem. In the meantime—"

"Why don't you get dressed, Hannah? We'll *both* go downstairs and see what we can work out."

"This is *my* room."

He twisted the card keys between his long, tapered fingers like a magician performing a sleight of hand. "But I've got the keys."

She sputtered, recognizing she'd been outmaneuvered—for the moment. She was entirely confident, however, that hotel management would see the situation *her* way.

Moving with caution so the towel wouldn't drop, she stepped into the closet, unzipped her hanging suitcase and pulled out some clothes. A Stetson rested on the top shelf.

Mentally, she groaned. It figured Holt Janson— with an *o*—would wear a *black* cowboy hat.

As she slipped into the bathroom, she heard him say in a cocky voice, "Nice view."

She didn't think he was looking out the window.

HOLT FINALLY let go of the full-blown smile that had been threatening for the last several minutes.

He hadn't been kidding about the view being great. Hannah Jansen—with an *e*—had a pair of terrific legs. And her fluffy white towel had done little to disguise her curvaceous figure. The whole time they'd been talking, he'd been bargaining with a higher power to make that towel come loose so he'd get an even better look. Obviously he hadn't made the stakes high enough.

Next time he might just try harder.

He wasn't, however, ready to risk the future of his Montana cattle ranch for a beautiful woman. He'd played that game once before and had lost, big-time. Holt Janson made it a point not to repeat his mistakes.

Ten minutes later when Hannah reappeared, Holt had to firmly remind himself of his vow.

Her honey-blond hair curled at her shoulders in a silken swirl that invited a man to touch it. She was dressed simply but elegantly in a loose-fitting blouse that tucked in at the belted waistband of hip hugging slacks. Wearing little makeup, and modest gold hoop earrings, she looked so damned innocent it almost made Holt laugh.

He hadn't been that naive since he was fourteen years old and his friend's mother had seduced him. That was twenty years ago.

Hannah, he guessed, had a half-dozen years to go before she saw her thirtieth birthday.

Somehow that made him feel old.

"WE ARE TRULY SORRY for this inconvenience, Mr. Janson. Miss Jansen." The hotel manager was thoroughly apologetic, but quite firm. There were no other rooms available. None. They would have to settle matters between them.

"There must be something," Hannah pleaded. "A rollaway bed in a closet?"

"Not even that, miss. They're all in use. I am sorry."

Holt leaned over the counter, his expression grim, his stance confrontational. "Where do you sleep, fella?"

The narrow-faced manager blanched. "Really, sir. There is no need for threats."

Placing a hand on Holt's arm, Hannah discovered rock-hard biceps beneath his Western-style shirt. A shiver of feminine awareness slid through her. "Come on," she said. She'd never been to Chicago before, but assumed public brawling, cowboy-style, was frowned upon in the better hotels. "We'll figure out something."

"Yeah. I guess we're stuck being roommates."

"That's not exactly what I meant."

They walked a few steps away from the front desk. The lobby was crowded with guests, most of them businessmen dressed in suits and ties. Holt stood out like a giant sequoia in a room full of potted plants.

He cupped her elbow. "At least the bed is plenty big enough for two."

"That's *precisely* not what I meant."

"I was afraid you'd feel that way," he said with a grin that tempted Hannah's better judgement.

As if he was used to having others obey his every whim, he ushered her through the lobby to a table near the piano bar. Before she could make any serious objection to his taking matters into his own hands, he'd ordered a beer. She agreed to a soft drink.

"Now, then, Hannah..." Leaning back in the club chair, he sipped his beer. "What's it going to take for you to let me have the room?"

"I'd rather discuss how you've decided to change your plans and no longer feel it necessary to be in Chicago."

"Can't do that. I'm here to see some bankers. Couldn't you see your way to taking your vacation another—"

"This is not a vacation. I'm here for the lingerie buyers' convention."

He cocked a single brow. "You sell lingerie?"

"I *design* lingerie and I've brought samples to show."

His gaze slowly—and with considerable precision—undressed her. "Lacy stuff?"

She swallowed thickly. "Yes."

"Maybe you'll let me take a look sometime."

"My sample case is in the room, though since I assume you don't represent a lingerie manufacturer, I hardly see that my designs would be of interest to you."

"Trust me on this, Hannah. I'd be *real* interested."

She hated the innuendo in his voice. She was a businesswoman and a fashion designer, albeit not yet a successful one. But someday—

She closed both hands around her icy glass. "We appear to be at an impasse."

"Yep. You could say that."

"I'm not going to budge out of Chicago until my business is successfully concluded."

"Neither am I. So I guess we'll just have to find a way to work together on this."

"And just how do you propose we do that?" she asked suspiciously.

"We're both adults. I'm sure I can count on you not to ravish me if we share the room."

A laugh caught in her throat. "But can I be sure the opposite is true?"

He held up one hand as though prepared to take a courtroom oath. "You have my absolute word of honor. Unless, of course, you change your mind and *want* me to ravish you. Then I'd consider—"

"Not likely, Mr. Janson."

"Call me Holt. Please."

He extended his hand to seal a bargain Hannah hadn't yet agreed to. Yet something in the tempting, teasing depth of his eyes—or maybe it was a secret longing buried within Hannah—made her accept his offer.

She desperately wanted to have an alternative to running her father's hardware store on into her own old age. Her lingerie designs could provide her with a way out, assuming she could break into a tight market.

Rooming with Holt Janson was simply a price she'd have to pay, and not an entirely unpleasant prospect, she admitted.

She did hope she wasn't making a terrible mistake, however.

"Good. I'm glad that's settled." Unfolding himself from the club chair that had looked too small for him, Holt stood. "I don't know about you, but I'm hungry. How 'bout we grab a bite in the coffee shop?"

"Just because we're—" the word jammed in her throat "—roommates, it doesn't mean you have to buy me dinner."

He smiled and his eyes crinkled at the corners. "Wasn't planning to, Hannah. Figured till we got to know each other a little better, we'd go Dutch treat—unless you'd like to buy."

Heat flamed her cheeks. She'd thought... "Dutch treat will be just fine, thank you," she said tautly. What a fool she felt. She should have recognized that a high-flying cowboy like Holt would have little interest in a small-town girl like her. Squaring her shoulders, she vowed not to make a gaffe like that again. She might not be very sophisticated, but she could fake it. Miss Aldridge, her high-school drama teacher, had once told her she was a darn good actress.

In the coffee shop, Holt ordered a medium-rare steak with all the trimmings. He made a point of asking for separate checks, sending Hannah a wickedly teasing wink as he did.

Hannah ordered a Cobb salad and a cup of decaf, her stomach already plenty unsettled by the cowboy sitting across from her.

Frantically searching for a topic of conversation

as they waited, she said, "So you're seeing some bankers tomorrow?"

"That's right. I'm trying to develop some new herds on my ranch."

"More cattle?"

The waitress brought two pots of coffee, one regular and one decaf. Deftly, she filled the two mugs.

"I've got enough head of beef for now," Holt said, nodding his thanks to the waitress. "I'm trying to broaden my base by getting into the gourmet-meat business—buffalo and venison."

"Really? Is the market that good?" Now she was sounding more cosmopolitan, possibly even an interesting conversationalist.

"Mostly the problem is the beef market has fallen off. The fact is, the deer-antler trade will probably be the most lucrative. At least in the beginning."

"What on earth for?"

His lips quirked into a smile. "Aphrodisiacs."

Hannah choked on a sip of coffee and coughed. "You're kidding," she sputtered. So much for being coolly urbane.

"Nope. I've got buyers lined up in California just waiting for me to produce in quantity. It seems ground-up antlers are big business in Japan and China."

"My heavens! Does it work?" As soon as she'd asked the question, Hannah wished she could snatch back her words. The gleam in Holt's eyes was downright sinful.

"I don't know," he drawled. "I've never felt the need to try the stuff." He poured two full teaspoons of sugar into his coffee and stirred it slowly. Provocatively. Gazing at Hannah the whole while. "Might be an interesting experiment—with the right woman, of course."

Hannah was confident Holt Janson didn't need any extra stimulation when it came to the opposite sex. And she sincerely hoped he wouldn't do any experimenting while they were sharing a room—a room with only one very large and inviting bed.

2

AFTER THEIR late dinner, Holt used his card key to let them back into their room. He shoved open the door and Hannah entered in front of him. A single light was on. The covers had been turned down on the bed and a chocolate mint was resting on each pillow.

Hannah shot a look of longing at the king-size bed.

"I'll take the love seat," she said with a sigh.

"You don't have to be a martyr. That bed's so big, you won't even notice I'm there." Holt would notice Hannah, though. He'd already discovered her unique fragrance during their dinner. It reminded him of the sweet, sharp scent of wildflowers in the spring.

"Sharing the same bed is definitely not part of our agreement," she said, shooting him a stern look. "There's an extra blanket in the closet, and I'll just steal one of the pillows—"

The phone rang.

Automatically, Holt reached for it.

"No!" Hannah cried. She dived for his hand,

knocking him back onto the bed and falling down beside him in the process.

"What's wrong with you?" He tried to untangle himself, but their legs were somehow wrapped around each other like soft pretzels.

"What if it's my father?" she hissed in a harsh whisper as though the caller could hear her. "Let me answer it."

"Hey, wait a minute. What if it's my lady friend?" That thought gave him pause.

"Oh. I didn't think—"

The phone rang again.

Frozen, they both stared at it.

She lifted her eyes—eyes the color of blue forget-me-nots—to meet his in an obvious plea for him to come up with a plan, any plan. For a moment he wanted to forget about the damn phone. Her leg was pressed against his thigh....

He gritted his teeth against the instinctive response of his body.

"Listen, I'll get it," he said. "If it's for you, I'll tell 'em they've got the wrong room. They'll call back and—"

"Then I'll answer it." She nodded toward the phone. "Good plan. Don't make them wait too long, or they'll get suspicious."

Holt picked it up on the third ring. "Hello."

Hannah squeezed her head right up close to his so she could hear, too.

Sweet, sexy prairie flowers.

There was a pause of several heartbeats before a male voice asked, "I was looking for Hannah Jansen."

She rolled her eyes.

"Sorry. They must have given you the wrong room," Holt said. As he cradled the phone, he heard the man's apology for disturbing him trailing off.

"Oh, pumpernickel!" Hannah muttered, her hands curling into fists.

"Such language! Who would have guessed?" Holt said, swallowing a laugh.

She nudged him hard with her elbow. "It's just that Dad is going to be upset. He hates making long-distance calls and now he'll have to dial again."

"Poor man. I'm filled with sympathy." He was also having a different reaction, one directly related to Hannah's elbow in his ribs and another soft, very intriguing part of her anatomy brushing against his arm.

The phone rang again.

She reached across him, and sweat began to bead on Holt's forehead.

"Hello." There was a long pause before she said in a voice that sounded slightly choked, "I'm sorry. They must have given you the wrong room." Visibly wincing, she replaced the phone in its cradle.

"Yeah?" he asked.

"A woman. She sounds very attractive."

He swore. "Adele. She probably expected me to call this evening. She knew I was coming into town."

"I'm sorry."

It was his own fault. He'd been rather distracted by Hannah Jansen since he'd arrived in Chicago. "She'll call back. She's a good sport."

The phone. Again.

He grabbed her hand before she could reach the receiver. Her porcelain skin was enticingly warm.

"We'll both listen without saying anything," he whispered. "Eventually the caller will say something and we'll know who it's for."

She nodded. "Got it." She lifted the phone and placed it between them. They were practically ear to ear.

A male voice asked, "Honey, is that you?"

"Of course, Dad. How are you? I didn't expect you to call so soon."

Ducking under the telephone cord, Holt moved away. He stripped off his shirt and hung it in the closet. Being roommates with Hannah Jansen was likely to pose more problems than he had anticipated. Admittedly, he'd given little thought to Adele in the equation. Nor had he suspected the impact Hannah would have on his libido.

As Hannah finished talking with her father, she noticed Holt had come out of the bathroom, his hair damp and curling at his nape. She was definitely going to ask for a clarification of the rules.

Neither of them should run around without a shirt on.

From what Holt had told her at dinner, he had acquired his broad chest and muscular physique through hard work on his Montana ranch. Evidently he'd also picked up a few scars in the process, unsettling souvenirs that managed to make his near physical perfection all the more tempting.

Even more disturbing, the light furring of whiskey-brown hair on his chest arrowed precisely toward a part of his anatomy that Hannah shouldn't be thinking about. She was truly grateful said part was still hidden by his jeans, though she was somewhat troubled by the fact he'd neglected to close the snap on his pants. *Careless man,* she thought, her breath snagging in her throat.

The phone rang yet again as Hannah's hand still rested on it.

"Careful," Holt warned.

Nodding, she lifted the phone so they could both listen, valiantly ignoring an impossibly strong desire to touch Holt's wonderfully masculine chest.

"Holt? Are you there?" a sultry feminine voice asked.

Hannah relinquished her hold on the phone, sternly reminding herself this roommate arrangement was temporary. She and Holt were simply making the best of an awkward situation. It was not her concern that a woman would call him. Or that he looked pleased with himself as he took the phone from her.

"Hi ya, babe. How's it going?"

Hannah was *not* going to eavesdrop, either.

"Sorry about that," he said to the caller. "I got, ah, tied up. There was a little mix-up here at the hotel."

Hannah moved away to give Holt some semblance of privacy. She went over to the closet, slipped her shoes off, placing them next to Holt's cowboy boots. Whimsically, she thought they made a nice-looking couple.

"No. Everything is fine... Now? Well, no, I'm kinda beat tonight. Long flight, you know. I thought maybe tomorrow night—"

She retrieved her toiletries from a side pocket in her hanging bag, then unzipped her bag and took out her nightgown and robe. With them in hand, she headed for the bathroom.

Holt, she noticed, had propped himself up on the bed with a couple of pillows at his back, his long legs stretched out in front of him. He was a man who was very comfortable with himself. She envied that.

When she came out a few minutes later, he was off the phone. He was still propped up on the far side of the bed but now there was a sheet pulled over the lower half of his body.

With a soft intake of air, Hannah's gaze slid to the jeans he'd tossed carelessly over a nearby chair.

Somehow she doubted he was wearing pajama bottoms. Nothing at all was more like it.

"There's still plenty of room in the bed," he said as she billowed out the spare blanket and draped it over the love seat. "If you want to change your mind."

"This will be fine." That was a lie, she realized. The couch was way too short for comfort, even for someone who had to stretch to make five foot four. But the alternative simply wasn't acceptable. "I hope my presence isn't going to cramp your style with Adele."

"I was wondering if we could do a little negotiating about that."

She raised her eyebrows. "She's someone you know rather, ah, well?"

"We've been friends for a long time." He tucked his arm behind his head and smiled at her across the room. "She's a dynamite lady, an attorney who is definitely on the fast track. If the cards fall right for her, I wouldn't be surprised to see her run for the U.S. Senate one of these days."

"Impressive." She fluffed up a pillow and placed it at one end of the couch. His taste in women was certainly admirable—not that she should care one way or the other. Nor would her two years of community college compete with a law degree.

"Both Adele and I have concluded we aren't cut out for marriage—to each other, or to anyone else. We've both been there, done that, and it didn't work out. But that doesn't mean that we don't en-joy—'' He speared his fingers through the thick, dark waves of his hair. ''I was hoping maybe you could find somewhere else to be tomorrow night, from say ten o'clock to midnight. She needs to be discreet.''

Heat raced to Hannah's cheeks. Her teeth clenched. ''I see.''

''Well, it's not like it's a one-night stand, you know. Adele and I—''

''I really don't want to know the intimate details of your private life, Mr. Janson.'' Knowing he had an inside track on the production of aphrodisiacs was bad enough.

''And I wouldn't have even brought it up if it weren't that we're sharing the same room. I was hoping you'd want to cooperate.''

''I'd be delighted.'' She crawled under the blanket and turned her back on him. Due to the short-ness of the couch, she was forced to draw her knees almost up to her chest. ''I promise I will be among the missing tomorrow night from ten to midnight. Assuming you're confident that will be sufficient time for whatever you have in mind.''

''You know darn well what I have in mind. And yeah, I'll make do. I figure you're paying half the room rent and have a right to get some sleep, too.''

''How *very* thoughtful of you.''

''I'll return the favor if you want to have a guy—''

"I don't."

"Why not? You got a boyfriend in Crookston?"

"No." She could have bitten her tongue off for admitting that so quickly.

"Why not?" he repeated more softly. "Seems to me a girl like you—"

"I'm not a *girl*. I'm twenty-eight years old, and perfectly happy being single. And I certainly don't pick up strange men when I'm visiting a new town." She huffed dramatically. "Now could you please turn off the light so we can both get some sleep tonight, since *your* activities are going to jeopardize our rest tomorrow."

There was an exceptionally long pause before the room went dark. An *angry* pause, she suspected.

"If you ask me," Holt said in a low voice edged with emotion, "the men in Minnesota must all be blind. If you lived in Montana, every cowboy for a hundred miles would be trying to hog-tie you."

In spite of herself, a warm surge of pleasure swept through Hannah. She knew Holt hadn't meant what he'd said, but he was very nice to have lied to her like that. She couldn't remember the last time a man had made her feel quite so feminine. Or desirable.

But then, she'd known every male in Crookston since the day she'd been born. Not one had held any particular appeal for her.

How ironic it was that a Montana cowboy who didn't believe in marriage and already had a girlfriend would be the first man she'd ever been strongly attracted to.

HOLT TOSSED aside one of the pillows and settled lower in the bed. There was no reason why he should have to defend his relationship with Adele. They had an understanding that worked for them. At least it had the last time he'd been in town, about a year ago.

A man had a right to seek out female companionship, didn't he? Twelve months of punching cattle, eating dust and fighting blizzards deserved a reward. And living twenty miles from the nearest place that could only marginally qualify as a town didn't provide many opportunities for socializing.

Which was just fine with Holt. Usually.

But he'd had an itch lately. He'd hoped Adele would be able to scratch it. Since he had to be in Chicago anyway, it made sense—

He glanced across the room at Hannah lying clearly uncomfortable on the couch.

Apparently where Hannah came from, men didn't get itches like the one that had been plaguing him. If they did, she'd be married and have a passel of kids by now.

Not that Holt had any interest in marriage.

But he did miss having a woman around. He liked the way they smelled. And how they looked in the morning, all sleepy-eyed and soft. He could even handle the mess they made in the bathroom.

Assuming they were willing to share the shower now and again.

He grinned.

Now there was an appealing thought Miss Jansen probably hadn't considered. Despite the temptingly sexy negligee she was wearing, she definitely appeared to be on the straitlaced side. Or maybe none of those jerks in Minnesota had taken it upon themselves to demonstrate to her the pleasures a man and woman could share.

It was hard to believe they'd miss a filly like Hannah. In addition to having really good lines, she had a lot of spirit. Holt liked that in a woman.

To his surprise, Hannah let out an audible sigh, stretched and stood. He grinned as the light from the window cut through the sheer fabric of her short nightgown and silhouetted her figure.

"So you've decided to share the bed after all?" he drawled.

"Certainly not. I'm going to fix the plumbing."

He blinked. She couldn't have said what he thought she'd said. "You're what?"

"Can't you hear it? The toilet has a leak and keeps on refilling. It's driving me crazy."

He'd been thinking about her luscious little body and *she'd* been thinking about the plumbing?

As if to prove the point, she walked into the bathroom and switched on the light.

"Couldn't that wait till morning?" he called to

her. He wondered if her makeup kit contained a wrench—in case of an emergency.

"I just turned off the water for now." As she returned, he caught another quick glimpse of her silhouette before the room went dark again.

He nearly groaned aloud. She was the sexiest plumber he'd ever seen. And that gown was like a gossamer cloud, something a man just naturally wanted to take his time removing.

The couch creaked as she settled down again. "It's like I thought. The handle is worn and needs to be replaced. I'll call maintenance in the morning."

"How you'd learn so much about plumbing?"

"Like I told you, my father owns a hardware store. It doesn't take a rocket scientist to handle simple household repairs. Women come into the store all the time thinking they have to hire a plumber or an electrician. Mostly they can take care of things themselves."

"My ex-wife wouldn't have known how to turn off the water, much less have any idea what was wrong."

"Maybe no one took the time to teach her."

Holt frowned. His ex hadn't been in the least interested in plumbing, or in much of anything else when it came to chores that needed doing around the ranch. Mostly she'd been bored to death living so far out of town. Having no one to socialize with, she'd taken up with one of his hired hands when his back was turned. The marriage had ended after that.

"So do you do electrical repairs, too?" he asked.

There wasn't any answer, only the soft sound of her steady breathing.

He was definitely losing his touch. His mind was conjuring up all sorts of interesting images of his roommate, and his body was responding to each and every one of them. *Painfully* responding.

Meanwhile, she wasn't giving him a single thought.

Some cowboy he was!

He'd been lying there staring across the room for a long time when she shifted on the couch and let out a soft groan of discomfort. Her breathing remained low and steady.

Damn, it was hell being a gentleman!

Reasonably confident she was sound asleep, he slipped out of bed. His one concession to modesty had been to leave his briefs on. He hadn't wanted either of them to be embarrassed.

In spite of heavy curtains on the window, the lights of Chicago crept into the room, casting a golden glow on Hannah, curled up on the couch.

Kneeling, Holt slipped his arms under her shoulders and knees. As he lifted her, the blanket slid away. She weighed less than most calves he'd hefted.

Carrying her with great care, he took her to the bed and lowered her onto it, then pulled the covers into place. Sighing, she stretched out and rolled onto her side.

He echoed her sigh. She was one hell of a sexy lady, whether she knew it or not.

Walking around the bed, he climbed in beside her. There was less distance between them than he'd expected. Her faint scent chased him to the edge of the mattress. His self-control teetered on a knife-edge.

Damn, this was going to be a long night.

Gritting his teeth, he thought about how he'd almost lost his ranch because of another woman, his ex-wife. He wasn't going to let that happen again.

Sometime before the morning light had invaded the room, he awoke. For a long, aching moment, he didn't know where he was.

A woman was sprawled across him, her lithe body draped over him, one leg hooked around his, and her breath warm against his cheek. She smelled of sweet prairie flowers. And sex.

His hand slid along her flank. Testing. Exploring. Learning territory that somehow felt familiar.

And then the damn alarm went off.

Hannah bolted upright. Or at least she tried to.

She was tangled up with something warm, firm and very masculine.

Silver-blue eyes looked up at her through thick, dark lashes. It was criminal the way men always got the best of the bargain when it came to—

"What are you doing in my bed?" she cried. She pushed herself away from Holt.

"Not a thing, sweetling. You're in *my* bed." His lazy drawl was morning-rough, just like his whiskers.

She blinked. He was right. This was *not* where she'd begun the night.

The alarm continued to blare.

Narrowing her eyes in accusation, she asked, "How did I get here?" She'd never been known to sleepwalk, certainly not into a man's bed.

With deliberate lack of concern, he reached for the clock radio, fiddled with it, finally quieting its incessant screeching.

Only then did she notice someone was pounding on the wall of the room next door.

"Apparently the neighbors aren't early risers," Holt said.

"Neither am I."

"Then why did you set the alarm?"

"I didn't. Five o'clock is definitely too early for me."

He eyed the dial on the clock radio and shrugged. "It's four in Montana. The cows aren't even up yet." He tugged the sheet up over his shoulder. "So let's catch another hour of sleep. What do you say?"

Sleep? With *him?*

She'd never in her life slept with a man. Well, she had now, she supposed, but she didn't actually remember it. So that didn't count. And it had only happened because she'd knocked herself out with a sleeping tablet during her brief journey to fix the plumbing last night. Better that, she had figured, than to lie awake all night thinking about the man she'd just slept with. Sort of.

Besides, at the moment, there wasn't a sleepy bone in her body. She'd never been more awake. Or more blatantly curious, she realized, her gaze sliding with interest down the length of him.

"If you decide to do more than look, let me know."

Her head snapped up. "In your dreams, Janson."

A teasing grin tilted his lips. "How did you guess? You were great."

"Oh, you—" She punched him on the shoulder. Though it wasn't a very effective blow, it did feel extraordinarily intimate. Playing in bed with a man was not a pastime she had expected to enjoy on this trip.

Nor should she be considering it now.

Twisting away, she hopped out of bed and snatched up the light robe that she'd draped across the back of the couch. No doubt about it, she had slept better last night next to Holt than she would have on the love seat—sleeping pill or not. In fact, she felt quite invigorated. It was going to be a good day.

A great day, in fact, to get her business off the ground.

3

HOLT'S EYES widened. "Do women in Minnesota really wear that stuff?"

"Of course they do. Why wouldn't they?"

He wasn't sure. But he knew damn well he'd never seen a woman in Montana strutting around in this kind of lacy underwear.

He'd taken his turn in the bathroom after Hannah, and when he came back into the bedroom he discovered she'd spread her lingerie samples across the bed. Just looking at all that silk and lace made his groin tighten.

Gingerly, he picked up a black, lacy thing that would scream "available" on any woman who wore it. "Do the men know?" His voice came out thick and hoarse.

"I suppose their husbands or boyfriends do."

"Then how the hell do they ever get any work done?"

She laughed a lighthearted sound that tickled his spine like a warm charge of electricity. "I take it you approve of my satin bustier design."

"Oh, yeah," he drawled. "I just wouldn't let any

woman of mine leave the house wearing a thing like this.''

"No one else would know."

"*But* I'd be walking around all day like a bow-legged cowboy."

She took the garment from him, her blue eyes twinkling with mirth, and placed it back in her sample case. "If you like it that much, that's a good sign. Most of the buyers are men."

"I can understand why." His gaze slid over Hannah. She'd pulled her hair back into a staid twist and her outfit looked all business, but he couldn't help wondering... "You wear your own designs?"

"Of course." She picked up a bit of red lace that didn't hardly look big enough to cover the tits on a fly.

He did a quick inventory of the bed. "Which ones?"

"I'm a pretty generous size, so I need a little underwire for support, but I insist on comfort. That's why I designed this." She handed him a bra made of satin and rose appliquéd net, simple and sexy, carrying a whiff of violets.

Swallowing hard, he tried to be as nonchalant as she was about the apparel she designed. But all he could think about was removing this same kind of bra from her sweet, lush body at a pace so leisurely it would drive her crazy. And him.

He fisted his hand around the soft fabric and imagined what it would be like.

"The whole idea," she went on as she repacked her bag, "is to find ways for women to feel both sexy and comfortable at the same time. The problem has been that men are the ones designing our undergarments, and they don't have to wear them. We have the same problem with shoes. The designers apparently don't give a fig about causing excruciating pain. Now that I think about it, I bet if a woman had designed that torture machine for mammograms a lot more of us would be willing to have our yearly checkups."

He stared at her blankly. How had the conversation gone from lingerie to mammograms? He'd never met a woman quite like Hannah. Her conversation flitted from one topic to the next so fast it made his head spin. Without any apparent effort, she had him off balance—in more ways than one.

"Could I please have my bra back?"

His gaze dropped to her breasts. Whatever an underwire was, it was doing its job real well. But he kinda wished she was wearing that bustier thing. Or maybe nothing at all.

"Yoo-hoo, Holt. Earth calling. I've got things to do, people to see. My bra, please." She held out her hand.

"Oh, sure. Right." Clearing his throat, he handed her back the bra in question, but not the one he was thinking about. "When you're ready, I'll go downstairs with you. I've got to see a couple of bankers this morning."

"Fine. I'll be just a minute."

Hurriedly, Hannah snapped her sample case shut. Though she tried not to show it, she was thoroughly flustered. It's not that she totally lacked knowledge about this man-woman thing. She was, after all, an avid reader of romance novels and knew the basics. She'd simply never put that information to the test.

Until now.

And as she had watched Holt handle her sample bra with his strong, callused hands, she'd all but felt him touching her. The imaginary sensation of his work-roughened palms skimming over her breasts, the power of his fingers squeezing her ever-so-gently, had sent heated messages right through her. In all those sensitive places normally confined by her bra, she'd felt him. *Wanted* to feel him, she admitted.

And in other places, too. Intimate places where no man had yet ventured.

The experience had left her slightly breathless, babbling about anything that came to mind, and determined to keep her distance from a man who could make her feel that way so easily. Lord, she didn't want to lose control of her life when she was so close to achieving the independence she'd been striving so hard to obtain.

Not that Holt was interested in hog-tying anyone. It seemed even he and his lady friend had an understanding about that.

Hannah would be well advised to remember both of those facts.

Grabbing the pull cord, Holt yanked open the window curtains. Morning sun poured through a sliding glass door that opened onto a balcony, and a breeze caught the sheer curtains, lifting them lightly. Beyond the dramatic Chicago skyline lay Lake Michigan, glistening in the sunlight.

"Oh, look at that poor bird," Hannah said.

Holt glanced at the gull perched on the short section of iron railing that separated their balcony from that of the one belonging to the adjacent room. "What's wrong with him?"

"His foot. One of his toes is missing. Poor baby."

He gave her a look that said she was being unduly sympathetic. "Captain Hook managed without a hand. I'm sure a bird can handle things with one less toe." He slid open the door, frightening the bird into flight, and stepped outside.

"No!" Hannah cried. Her stomach did a flip-flop. "Don't go out there."

"Why not?"

"We're twenty floors up, that's why not!" The man was crazy. They were hundreds and hundreds of feet up in the air. She could hardly bring herself to peer over the edge, much less walk out there.

"It's perfectly safe." He jumped up and down to prove his point.

Hannah's palms began to sweat profusely.

"Afraid of heights, are we?" He grinned at her, looking as pleased with himself as a sixth-grade boy who'd managed to gross out a girl with some stupid, macho stunt. Which he had.

"If you must know, I'm terrified of anything higher than a stepladder."

"Too bad. The lake looks great from out here." Stepping back inside, he left the curtains fluttering in the breeze and said, "So, are you ready to get on with the day?"

"Gladly."

With relief, she hefted her sample case off the bed to the floor, tipped it back so it would roll on two wheels and made sure the decorative Hannah's Frills labels would be obvious on all sides.

"I'm ready," she announced.

"Then let's go conquer Chicago." Holt picked up his Stetson and held the door open for her.

Allowing her to exit first, he eyed her very attractive derriere with interest and admired the gentle sway of her clingy skirt brushing her legs an intriguing inch above her knees. He wondered if, in addition to that sexy bra, Hannah might also be wearing one of her minuscule designs for underpants. The high-cut kind that made a woman's legs look like they went on forever. Red ones, he thought. Or maybe the same rich, creamy shade as her skin. As soft as dew on a rose petal, he recalled.

Little wonder, after examining her samples, he'd needed to step outside to cool off.

The door to the adjacent room opened and a woman of striking proportions swept out. Her gray hair was piled on top of her head and her navy-blue suit looked just this side of an admiral's uniform. She gave Hannah a scathing look, then included Holt in her haughty sweep of disapproval.

"I trust tomorrow morning my sleep will not be disturbed at such an early hour." She lifted her head regally and proceeded down the corridor in front of them.

"We're sorry," Hannah said to the woman's rigid back. "Really. We had no idea—"

But the woman wasn't listening. She reached the open doors of the elevator first, stepped inside, and effectively blocked their entrance. The doors slid closed, leaving only an unpleasant memory of her stern face.

Holt jammed his finger on the call button but it was too late. "Man, has she got nerve," he complained.

"More than you know. That was Bubbles Von Hemmelrich. In the trade papers, they call her the Corset Queen. She's very influential in the industry."

"Bubbles?" He nearly choked.

"*Ms.* Von Hemmelrich to us peons, and then with a slight bow at the waist, if you please. It's not considered good business to get on the wrong side of her."

"And we just did?"

Hannah slanted him a glance and sighed. "I think that happened when the alarm went off this morning."

"Hey, don't let her get you down. Her stays were probably poking her, and that put her in a bad mood." Lifting Hannah's chin, he gave her an encouraging smile. "You'll knock 'em dead with your designs. I promise."

"I hope you're right."

A slight tremble of her full lips snagged his attention. Knowing he was partly to blame for not getting that stupid alarm turned off fast enough, he wanted to bolster her spirits. That was all he intended as he dipped his head toward hers.

What he got was a taste of heaven.

The flavor reminded him of a cherry pie fresh from the oven; the texture was soft satin, like the garments she designed.

He backed off in a hurry. A man could develop a dangerous hunger for a sweet morsel like Hannah Jansen. Holt knew better than to risk getting too attached to her particular flavor. It was too likely to become habit-forming.

There was a startled look in her forget-me-not eyes, as though she'd been caught off guard as much as he had.

Vaguely, he was aware of the ping announcing the elevator's return and the doors opening. But he couldn't quite drag his gaze away from her.

Her tongue slid out to moisten her lips.

Deep in his gut, he felt a tightening.

"The elevator is here," she said, still holding his gaze.

He blinked, trying to undo the spell that had him mired in quicksand, unable to move. "Yeah, right."

Turning, he had to jam his hand between the doors to keep them from closing.

They rode down to the lobby, both facing front. They didn't speak. Holt sure as hell didn't know what to say, assuming he could even manage a coherent thought. No woman was supposed to taste that good.

When the doors opened, she managed to get her feet moving before he could even budge. She bumped her sample case out the door. One wheel stuck in a grove and she gave the case a quick kick with her foot, latch high. Dragging it behind her over the threshold, she headed into a lobby filled with milling businessmen and women. She'd gone twenty feet before Holt could get his own act together enough to move.

Then he noticed the latch on her sample case had sprung open. A trail of frilly lace and silk dribbled out behind the case labelled Hannah's Frills.

"Hannah!" He hurried after her, scooping up a pair of shocking-pink undies, one of those black bustier things, and a gingham G-string with garters, for God's sake. He hadn't seen—

"Nice trail of bread crumbs," a bystander commented dryly amid an increasing murmur of laughter in the lobby. Every man was looking in Holt's direction. Or Hannah's.

"Hannah!" he said again, stooping to pick up a pair of rubber falsies that had bounced to the tile floor all tangled in yellow eyelet.

A gossamer cloud of blue billowed from the case.

"Hannah!" he shouted.

Finally she stopped and turned. Her eyes widened. "Oh, my!"

The chuckles rose in volume.

Figuring his face was about as red as it could get, Holt shoved all of the undies into her arms. "I think you dropped something."

"Oops." Her eyes sparkled with mischief. "It looks like a lot of the buyers got a preview of Hannah's Frills."

"They sure as hell did." Catching something like glee in her tone, he gazed at her suspiciously. "I don't suppose you spilled all that stuff on purpose, did you?"

"Me?" She batted her eyes in a way that wasn't in the least innocent. "Now how on earth would a little girl from Minnesota farm country come up with a marketing idea like that?"

He shot a look at the fancy Hannah's Frills lettering on the case, something every buyer in the lobby would have noticed. Repressing a laugh that would have given the joke away, he shook his head. "And here I was worried Bubbles would blackball you."

"She still may," Hannah agreed, sobering. "But if I go down, I intend to do it a blaze of glory."

Holt concluded the only way Hannah was going was up. To the very top of the heap. "Watch out, Bubbles," he said softly and with considerable pride. He touched a fingertip to Hannah's upturned nose. "A new queen is about to be born."

HANNAH CLASPED Holt's words of encouragement close to her heart as she set up her displays in the booth she'd rented for the trade show. His kiss she tried not to think about, or the way he had touched her.

The man was having another woman up to their room tonight, she reminded herself. A sultry attorney who was probably as gorgeous as she was smart.

"I presume you are Hannah?"

Her head snapped up at the sound of the imperious voice. "Yes, ma'am...Ms. Von Hemmelrich."

The older woman fingered a spandex bra-slip with mild interest. "Your little exhibition in the lobby this morning was quite effective."

"Thank you." Hannah saw no reason to dissemble. She wasn't about to fool Bubbles anyway.

"I might have tried a stunt like that myself, thirty or forty years ago."

"I'll take that as a high compliment, Ms. Von Hemmelrich."

"Don't. Compliments don't pay the bills. Only orders count, not words." With casual indifference, she studied a lace corset. "Where do you get your boning?"

"From my supplier."

Bubbles cocked a critical brow. "I see you are not quite as naive as I had first thought."

"I'd be happy to discuss design-licensing arrangements, if you'd be interested."

"We have in-house designers."

"Yes, I know. But they've been cutting corners lately and haven't been keeping up with the needs of the younger generation. Young women these days are far more athletic than they used to be and want more freedom of movement, even when they dress up."

Her eyes narrowing in a show of disdain, Bubbles dropped the corset back onto the table. "How clever of you to point that out," she said icily. "Beginners are always so confident at their first trade show, but they soon learn the business isn't often kind to first-timers." She dipped her head in an arrogant salute. "Do give my regards to your husband. I'm sure he'll be pleased to have his little lady back in the ranch kitchen where she belongs."

"He's not—" Hannah clamped her mouth shut even as anger flushed her cheeks. She didn't want to get into a discussion with the Corset Queen about her marital status, or the fact that her roommate was a virtual stranger. She wasn't anybody's "little lady" and certainly wouldn't appreciate that label if she were married.

Which wasn't likely to happen any time soon, given her limited choices in Crookston. Not that it mattered.

Glaring at Von Hemmelrich's departing figure, Hannah sincerely wished one of the stays in Bubbles's massive corset would snap and give her a goose right where—

"You hung in there real good with the Queen."

Hannah turned toward the man in the adjacent booth. Thin-faced, middle-aged and balding, he was smiling at her. She smiled back. "Am I allowed to say thank you?"

"You bet, Hannah. Anybody who can stand toe-to-toe with that ol' witch and not get too bloodied is my kind of person. I'm Sam Spivak, by the way." He extended his hand. "Fanfare Follies out of Philly. We make the best silicone-lined stay-up stockings in the country."

"It's a pleasure to meet you, Mr. Spivak." As they shook hands, Hannah decided it felt good to have a friend in the business.

Sam Spivak turned out to be a friend and more. As the day wore on, he urged his buddies to visit Hannah's booth and check out Hannah's Frills. It seemed as though he knew everyone in the trade. She passed out more business cards than she could count and gave her spiel to dozens of prospective manufacturers as well as retailers interested in carrying new lingerie lines.

If no contracts were immediately offered, it didn't matter. At this point the important thing was to generate interest in her designs. In time, her designs would prove themselves.

BY LUNCHTIME Holt was less sure about getting the expansion loan he needed than he had been when he'd arrived in Chicago. He was also beginning to question the business sense of the local bankers.

"I'm sure you're aware, Mr. Edwards, that there's been a serious decline in the consumption of beef over the last few years."

Without looking up, Rod Edwards sliced another bite of rare prime rib and slapped it with a dollop of horseradish. The upscale restaurant was filled with businessmen making deals. The whole scene made Holt feel claustrophobic and eager to get back to the wide-open spaces of Montana.

Or to the cozy hotel room he shared with Hannah, he thought with odd sense of anticipation. He'd had a devil of a time all morning keeping thoughts of her out of his head so he could concentrate on the business at hand.

"I'm afraid our bank has no fiscal experience underwriting the raising of buffalo or deer," Edwards said. He finished off his glass of red wine and signaled the waiter for another. "If you could provide us with the names of other financial institutions that have made similar loans, and some indication of repayment records, that would be helpful.''

If Holt had known where else he could get a loan, he would have gone there first. And not wasted his time with a dolt like Edwards, or the competing banker who had turned him down that morning. Montana bankers had already been a washout; too many of the state's ranches were struggling.

''Specialty gourmet meats are a growing industry, Mr. Edwards. For instance, ostrich steaks are going for seven dollars a pound at retail these days.''

Edwards stared at him through the thick lenses of his bifocals. ''Then why don't you raise ostriches?''

Holt was not going to lose his temper. Edwards was about as dense as a banker could be, but he hadn't given him a flat ''no.'' Yet.

''Ostriches don't exactly thrive in below-zero weather,'' Holt pointed out as patiently as he could. ''On the other hand, Montana is the natural habitat for buffalo and deer. The meat is extremely flavorful and there can be some lucrative by-products. Have you ever tasted venison, Mr. Edwards?''

''Nope. I'm strictly a beef and potatoes man. The wife is always trying to get me to eat more chicken, but my answer is always the same. Where's the beef?''

''The Beef Council thanks you, I'm sure,'' Holt

mumbled, fascinated by the way Edwards's double chin wattled when he laughed at his own joke.

Pulling a glossy folder from the slender briefcase he carried, Holt said, "I've put together a business plan that I think makes sense, Mr. Edwards. I'd appreciate your taking a look at it."

"Be happy to. I'll have to talk to some of my associates, of course. It will be a day or two before I can get back to you."

"I understand. I'm staying at the Towers downtown."

Using a piece of roll, Edwards sopped up the last of the meat juice on his plate. "I'll be in touch."

His promise didn't carry much enthusiasm.

At least Holt had Adele to look forward to this evening. His trip to Chicago wouldn't be a total waste.

Except when he thought of Adele, another face popped into his mind—one with a turned-up nose, blue eyes and honey-blond hair. A woman who was wearing only a towel and a shocked expression.

HANNAH CHECKED her watch.

She'd lingered over drinks with Sam and some of his cronies after they'd closed down their booths for the day. But now she wanted to get upstairs, have a quick shower, and get out of the room before Holt showed up with his lady friend.

She gritted her teeth against the uncalled-for surge of possessiveness she felt toward her roommate. He was a big boy—a *very* big boy—and perfectly free to dally with a woman, if that's what he wanted. Assuming it was okay with the woman.

Which it wouldn't be for Hannah.

Chalk it up to midwestern standards, if you like, but Hannah wasn't about to go to bed with guy unless she was in love. *Deeply* in love. So far that hadn't happened.

Not that she hadn't hoped it would.

On soft summer nights she'd been known to watch the fireflies and dream of a stranger driving into town. He would sweep her off her feet and certainly take her away from the dull reality of handling the books for a hardware store, however much she might dearly love her father, and the town, too.

But even a small-town Minnesota girl could dream, couldn't she?

After telling Sam she might see him later, she hurried upstairs.

There was no sign that Holt had been back to the room.

She parked her sample case back in the closet and began shedding her clothes as she went into the bathroom.

"Oh, shoot!" she muttered.

She'd forgotten to call maintenance about the leaking toilet. With a groan, she realized it wouldn't be fair if Holt and his lady friend had to listen to the darn thing hiss while they were trying to—

Well, she didn't want to think about the specifics

of what they were going to do. But it did seem only thoughtful that she get the toilet fixed before he came back.

She picked up the phone on the nightstand, checked for the maintenance department and punched in the number. It rang—once, twice, three times. Apparently the maintenance people were either otherwise occupied or didn't work this late in the evening. Which didn't solve the problem of a leaking toilet that would surely be a distraction when Holt and his lady friend were doing... whatever.

Tugging on her clothes again, Hannah hurried out the door and downstairs.

The desk clerk was no help at all. She doubted he even knew what the innards of a toilet looked like, much less how they worked.

Undaunted, she made her way to the basement.

There wasn't a maintenance worker in sight, but she did find a toolbox that had been left open, which was surprising since most workmen were terribly protective of their own tools.

Picking up what she needed, including some replacement parts she found on a nearby shelf, she hurried upstairs. The hour was growing late. She'd have to move quickly if she was going to fix the toilet and have time for her shower, too.

The plumbing project didn't go quite as easily as she had hoped. It never did, she mused, as she set aside the tools and stripped for her shower.

The sound of feminine laughter stopped her with one foot in the tub and one foot still on the tile floor. Breathlessly, she froze in place.

The laughter came again, closer, this time echoed by a familiar male voice.

She cursed under her breath. He'd come back early. At least a half hour too early.

Now what was she going to do?

4

"I TOLD YOU, for Italian food in Chicago, you can't beat Giovanni's." With an easy aura of sophistication, Adele crossed the room and dropped her purse on the bedside table. She was a strikingly chic woman with a dramatic profile and dark hair that never showed a strand out of place—not even after making love, as Holt recalled.

As she turned back to him, a confident smile of anticipation lifted her perfectly sculpted lips. "Besides, a good dose of garlic always does wonderful things for my libido. How about you?" Her voice dropped to a sultry purr on the question.

"Yeah, sure. Great restaurant." Hedging his response with a troubling lack of enthusiasm, Holt's gaze swept the room. No sign of Hannah. That was good, he told himself as he hooked the Do Not Disturb sign over the outside knob before letting the door close. She'd get the message if she came back early—he hoped. No way did he want to be interrupted while he and Adele were—

His gaze snapped to the bed—to Hannah's side of the bed—and the image of the two them tussling together that morning popped into his head. His body reacted with surprising force to the memory.

Damn, he shouldn't be thinking about that!

"Hmm." Cocking her head, Adele sniffed genteelly. "What a delightful room freshener they're using. Wildflowers, isn't it? They must know you're from the prairies of Montana."

Holt closed his eyes. That was Hannah's sweet, innocent scent, all right, teasing at his own misbehaving libido, which seemed unable to focus on his date for the night. How the hell was he supposed to make love to Adele when with every breath he'd catch another woman's fragrance? A woman whose image and fierce determination to succeed had been tormenting him all day.

When he opened his eyes he discovered Adele had removed her suit jacket, revealing a black slip with a narrow band of lace across the top. The sight should have made him hard. In the past, it always had.

But not tonight.

Instead he examined the garment with a critical eye. Hannah's designs were sexier, more feminine, without actually being any more revealing. *How do you suppose she does that?* he wondered. *There must be a real art to designing...*

"Holt? That's the third time tonight you've drifted off to another planet. Is something wrong?" Her fingers paused at the button on the waistband of her formfitting skirt.

"Oh, ah, sorry. It must be the time change." Emptying the coins from his pockets onto the desk, Holt played for time. Adele deserved better than a distracted lover. And at the moment, that's exactly was he was—distracted.

He heard a small, feminine cough.

Glancing over his shoulder, he asked, "Are you okay?"

She looked at him blankly. "I'm fine. Are *you* coming down with something?"

"No, not me." He pulled his wallet out of his back pocket and placed it with the change on the desk.

"Maybe you're more upset about not getting the loan than you thought you were."

"Possibly."

Closing the distance between them, Adele rested a caring hand on his cheek. Her fingers felt cool. "I know a banker or two in town. Why don't I pull some strings and see if I can get you an appointment?"

"Hey, that'd be great, but I hate to impose."

She smiled and brushed a quick kiss on his lips. "What are friends for?"

Somewhere nearby an object clattered onto a tile floor.

Adele arched her brows.

Suspicion prickled Holt's spine. "The walls are real thin in this hotel."

"Hmm. Then we'll have to be very quiet, won't

we?'' she whispered, unbuttoning the top two buttons of his shirt as she backed him closer to the desk. ''Though if you're as good as you've always been, that won't be easy for me.''

Though he was bolstered by the compliment, Holt wasn't sure whispering would help.

Someone muffled a sneeze. Unless she was a damn good ventriloquist, it hadn't been Adele. And it sure as hell hadn't been Holt.

His gaze shot toward the closed bathroom door. ''Look, Adele, I've gotta...give me a minute, will you?''

Sidestepping away, he gave her an unconvincing grin. He shoved open the bathroom door, stepped inside, closed the door behind him and flicked on the light.

Except for the slight flutter of the shower curtain, the room appeared empty. The big wrench sitting on the closed toilet seat suggested appearances could be misleading, however.

He yanked open the shower curtain.

With a bundle of clothes bunched in front of her naked body, Hannah lifted her big forget-me-not blue eyes to meet his.

His body's reaction was swift and all too predictable. ''Don't you ever wear any clothes?'' he hissed.

''I was going to take a shower.''

''Now? You were supposed to make yourself scarce.''

"I was going to, but you came back early."

"Not that early, for God's sake. We had an agreement."

"I was fixing the toilet. I didn't want you to be disturbed—"

"Disturbed?" He fought to keep his voice low. "What the devil do you think you're doing now? Adele's out there wondering what the hell is going on."

"I'm sorry." She blinked rapidly, her blond lashes like furious little fans brushing against the high color of her cheeks. "I was trying to get dressed and I knocked your shaving kit off the counter. And then it was so cold in here because someone had turned up the air conditioner, I started to shiver. That's when I sneezed. So you see, I wasn't trying to disturb—"

Adele knocked on the door. "Holt, honey, are you all right?"

"I'm…fine," he called through the door, choking on the words. Nothing about this evening had gone quite right, and now he was getting a hard-on looking at the *wrong* woman.

"You go ahead and do…whatever," Hannah told him in a whisper. "I'll be still as a mouse. I promise."

He rolled his eyes. "I can't— I mean, with you here, I couldn't—"

"Holt, shall I call room service and get you

something to settle your stomach?'' Adele asked with concern. ''Maybe you had too much—''

''No!''

Hannah winced.

''I don't need anything for my stomach.'' But he was developing a severe pain right at the back of his skull, all because of a bad case of frustration brought on by a minx of a woman who liked to double as a plumber and was wearing nothing more than gooseflesh and a sorrowful expression.

''Maybe we should just explain to her—''

''Oh, right,'' he groaned. ''Adele will love it that we're sharing a room. Maybe if you were ugly as sin—''

''You don't think I'm ugly?''

''Of course not. You're the sexiest woman—'' He scowled.

Her smile brought a guileless sparkle to her eyes.

''Now look...'' he muttered.

''Holt, honey, maybe I ought to go on home,'' Adele said through the bathroom door. ''We can get together tomorrow when you're feeling better.''

''No, wait!'' He wasn't about to be bamboozled out of the grand finale he'd planned for his night on the town. He'd already missed out on Adele the prior evening, and he only got to Chicago about once a year, if that. He'd known Adele for years and when they were together—

Someone pounded on the wall of the adjacent room.

"Bubbles!" Hannah's hand flew to her mouth and her eyes went wide with horror.

Holt swore long and with considerable feeling.

Adele opened the bathroom door. Her gaze skipped with interest from Holt to Hannah and back again. "This ought to be a really good one."

"It's not what you think, Adele," Holt asserted.

Hannah blurted out, "I was trying to fix the plumbing. We don't even know each other. Not really." She shivered and hugged her wad of clothes more tightly to her chest—which didn't do a thing to hide her sexy, bare legs.

Adele's brows arched incredulously.

"I think I'll just flush myself down the toilet," Holt mumbled. "Now that you've done such a terrific job of *fixing* it."

To her credit, Adele turned with great dignity—particularly since she was only wearing a slip and high heels—and walked back into the bedroom.

Holt shot Hannah a withering look that had been known to sober up drunken cowboys. All he got from Hannah was a slight shrug of her creamy white shoulders.

"I'll just wait here awhile."

"You've got that damn straight. And put some clothes on, will you? I've got about ten thousand acres worth of fences to mend with Adele."

ALMOST AN HOUR later, barefoot but dressed in her skirt and blouse, Hannah poked her head out the bathroom door. She'd stayed inside while Holt and Adele had a rather thorough—and sometimes loud—discussion about her presence, interspersed with an occasional thump on the wall from the room next door.

"Is she gone?" she asked the man who lay stonily on the big bed, his shirt open to bare his chest, his hands stacked behind his head. Her eyes darted to his Western-cut slacks where they stretched tautly across his pelvis.

"Yeah, she's gone."

"I'm sorry, really I am."

"Don't apologize, not again."

"Is she super, *super* mad at you?"

"Naw, she's a good sport. She understands it was just a mix-up."

"I'd be furious," she mumbled under her breath. Clearly, Adele was far more understanding than Hannah would have been if her lover had been rooming with another woman. There evidently was a world of difference in attitudes between Crookston and Chicago.

"Maybe we ought to try again to find separate rooms," she suggested. "You'll still be in town for a night or two."

"I already thought of that. It's still a no-go."

Hannah lifted her chin at the unexpected blow to her ego that he was so eager to move out. For heaven's sake, she'd suggested the idea herself. It was only reasonable—

Settling on the side of the bed next to the phone, she yanked open a drawer of the bedside table, where she expected to find the phone book. There *had* to be some hotel, or maybe a scuzzy motel, that had a room available.

Her eyes widened. There wasn't a phone book in the drawer, but there was—

"Chocolate?" she questioned, her voice catching as she stared at the neat foil packets of condoms in the drawer.

"Huh?"

"I, ah, didn't know they came in flavors."

Her comment propelled Holt into motion. "Geez, Hannah, why are you snooping?" He slammed the drawer shut.

"I *wasn't* snooping. I was looking for the telephone book."

"At this time of night? Who're gonna call? The pizza man?"

"I was trying to find another hotel room." She folded her arms across her chest. "I've heard most women really like chocolate. It's something about endorphins."

"Lay off, Hannah. It was supposed to be a joke. Add a little variety, you know."

"I've been known to eat a whole quart of rocky-road ice cream by myself."

He groaned, clearly exasperated with her.

She was kind of tickled. And fascinated. "What other flavors do they come in?"

"How the hell would I know?"

"I just thought there might be a market for—"

His arm snaked around her waist and he flattened her to the bed. Suddenly he was above her, big and strong and totally intimidating. A frisson of exquisite pleasure shot through her. Is this how it felt to be ravished by—

Looking up at him, she felt her body go entirely still. His eyes were as black as sin—and *sin* was exactly what she was thinking about. Stroking that powerful chest of his, running her fingers through the springy hair that so tempted her. Exploring the shape and heat of his lips, tasting him. Feeling the weight of him press down on her in ways she'd only imagined. Experiencing for the first time—

"Damn it, Hannah! Don't look at me that way."

"What way?" she complained with a breathless sigh, her mouth dry, her respirations coming as fast as if she'd run the 10K charity race along the Red River Lake dike at Crookston.

"Like you want me for dessert."

Is that how she was looking at him? She did feel rather like a cat eager to lap up a warm bowl of milk. Except she suspected Holt's flavor would be far more tangy.

"I already had dinner," she told him.

His eyes narrowed. "With who?"

She tried to shrug but he had her nailed in place. Broad shoulders. Strong arms. A lean torso without an ounce of fat. And narrow, cowboy hips that pressed into her.

She swallowed hard and licked her lips. "With a man I met at the show."

His blue-black eyes followed the motion of her tongue with amazing interest. "Is he married?"

"How should I know? We talked about lingerie. He works for Fanfare Follies out of Philly. They make—"

"I don't even want to know." Exasperated, Holt rolled off her onto his back. *Fanfare Follies?* His imagination filled in all the blanks he wanted to think about, assuming he was able to think at all.

How could a woman be so naive? And make him so hot at the same time? Not that it would do him a damn bit of good.

Hannah Jansen—with an *e*—was about as far off-limits as any woman could be. If she'd been a few years younger, he would have called her jailbait. As it was, she was a trap any man in his right mind would have enough sense to avoid. Sure as hell, a sane man wouldn't end up rooming with her in a plush hotel in a strange city where she was miles away from her mama and her shotgun-toting old man.

Get real!

Holt Janson—with an *o*—was in deep trouble. A few thousand miles wouldn't stop her father from tracking him down if Holt did what he was thinking about. And he was thinking about it—*real* hard. *Hard* being the operative word.

Hannah sighed, troubled by the odd way she wished Holt hadn't lifted his weight away from her. "I guess if Adele isn't coming back—"

"She's not. We're going to do lunch tomorrow."

"I'll stay out of the room," she quickly announced, mortified that she might interrupt Holt's romantic interlude a second time. "I promise, I won't come anywhere near—"

"Not *that* kind of lunch!"

"Oh." Hannah understood how upset he was, but she simply didn't know what to do about it. Or what to do about the heat that was thrumming through her veins. Holt's heat, she suspected. "In that case, if you're sure there aren't any other rooms—"

"There aren't."

"Then I'll just get ready for bed."

He didn't say anything as she found her nightgown and went into the bathroom to change. When she returned, he was still on the bed, but now he had the quilt pulled up over him, hiding that incredible chest of his.

She reached for the spare blanket.

"I don't want you sleeping on that dinky couch."

"I don't mind."

"You'll toss and turn all night, and drive me crazy." He looked at her from beneath half-lowered lids. "I'm sleeping on top of the sheet. You sleep underneath and I'll guarantee your virtue will remain intact."

At the moment, that particular attribute was one Hannah put less store in than she had only days ago.

She eyed the couch, weighing her choices. She'd be miserable trying to sleep there and might well keep Holt awake. That hardly seemed fair when she'd already ruined his evening.

"Come on, Jansen with an *e*. It's late. I've gotta get my sleep."

Surrendering to the temptation of the big bed, and Holt's nearness, she admitted, Hannah turned off the light and gingerly slid between the cool sheets. She shivered lightly as she inhaled Holt's masculine scent. She'd had no idea just the aroma of a male could be so arousing.

She lay there looking up at the ceiling, watching the faint shifting of light from the curtained window and listening to him breathe. The sound was at once disturbing and comforting. Perhaps it was simply the closeness of another human being when she was a long way from home that caused her to want to snuggle toward him. But she resisted the impulse.

Because of the late hour, she hadn't wanted to take another sleeping pill for fear she would oversleep in the morning. She still had her designs to sell, her new independence to create. Being a no-show at her own booth would hardly make a professional statement about her commitment to her career.

Muttering something unintelligible, Holt shifted on the bed.

Hannah held her breath. She wasn't in the least bit sleepy. With a superior act of will, she clamped down on the errant thought that he might roll over and take her in his arms. Kiss her. Make love to her. Again and again…

No! She reeled in her fantasy before it got entirely out of hand. He was an honorable man and he'd promised that her worthless virtue would stay intact. Besides, there was no way she could compete with a sophisticated woman like Adele. Holt would probably laugh at her if he knew what she'd been thinking.

He flopped over again, this time rocking her side of the bed.

"Are you asleep?" she whispered.

"Not likely."

"Neither am I."

He snorted. "Glad to hear you don't talk in your sleep."

She let a few beats of silence go by, wondering if he'd say anything else, wishing she could listen to his deep baritone voice forever and knowing that wasn't in the cards. Not for a small-town Minnesota girl and a Montana cowboy.

"Tell me about Montana," she asked so softly that if he'd fallen asleep it wouldn't disturb him.

"My ranch, you mean?"

"Yes. I've never been West." Though she'd certainly read plenty of romance novels based in the Big Sky country.

After a pause, he said, "There are rolling hills that stretch as far as the eye can see. Sometimes there's not even a tree that breaks the horizon. The springtime's the best. The grassland's green and lush, and you can taste it like sugar candy on your tongue. And the smell…wildflowers everywhere."

Smiling, Hannah listened enthralled. He was so poetic, so obviously proud of his land and his ranch, she could see what he saw, smell the sweet scents of his home, even the more pungent aroma of herds of beef cattle on the move. She sweated in the summer with him, froze in the blizzards of winter. And wished she could be there with him helping to drag bales of hay to stranded cattle when they were shoulder-deep in drifting snow.

"How 'bout you?" he asked after a while.

She blinked. "Me?"

"Minnesota. What's it like?"

"Oh, quiet, I guess, like Montana. Except we always seem to have the hum of tractors plowing or planting or harvesting. Sugar-beet farmers, mostly, where I come from."

"Big town?"

"The sign outside of town says eight thousand, but I'd guess that's wishful thinking on the part of the town fathers. We're near Grand Forks, though. We think of them as city slickers.''

He chuckled, a low rough sound. "I've got to go twenty miles to find a town that's not even half that size.''

"Do you have family?" she asked, teetering precariously close to even more intimacy.

"A sister. She's an attorney in San Francisco. She hated the ranch.''

"I've got a younger brother in the navy. He didn't have any interest in Dad's hardware store, so he enlisted right out of high school. A lot of midwestern boys do that. He's stationed in San Diego now and has a wife and a baby. I miss him." And tried hard not to resent that he'd been able to pursue his own dreams.

"Meanwhile, you're stuck in Crookston?"

"It's not so bad," she said defensively. "After Mother died, Dad needed someone to help out at the store.''

"And take care of him?"

She bristled at his implied criticism. "I love him very much. He's always been a wonderful father.''

"Yeah, sure. But that doesn't stop you from wanting your own life, does it?"

No, it didn't. But it didn't mean she hated Minnesota, either, or her father. And the hardware store only a little.

He shifted again, turning toward her, Hannah thought.

"I was married for a while," he said. "Like my sister, she couldn't stand living so far away from the action. Montana can be a very lonely place."

Hannah swallowed hard. "So can Minnesota."

"I'm not planning to try marriage again." His voice was low and rough and very determined. "The first time nearly cost me the ranch."

In the silence that followed, the numbers on the digital clock flopped over. Outside, a siren wailed, muted by the twenty floors they were above street level.

"I don't want you to think I'm hitting on you," he said in his deep, rough voice, "but if I don't kiss you, I'm never going to get any sleep."

Her heart lurched. "Under the circumstances, one kiss wouldn't be too awful."

"One."

With unerring accuracy in the darkness, he claimed her mouth. He was moist heat and rose petals and a sweet taste of heaven. He was no inexperienced farm boy like those she had kissed furtively at the front door or in the back seat of a car at the drive-in. Holt's kiss swept through Hannah like a spring tornado. She wanted his earthiness but knew it was far more than she could possibly handle. Or match.

But he'd set a different kind of a match to the banked coals of her sexuality. Staid, proper Hannah Jansen realized for the first time what she'd been missing—what all the fuss was about. Or at least she was getting a glimpse of what the flame could do.

When he slid his tongue along the seam of her lips, she felt herself open for him like a prairie flower at the first blush of spring sunshine. Her body clenched—all over. She heard a low, throaty murmur of pleasure and knew the sigh had been hers.

He broke the kiss with a groan. She wanted to protest. She wanted *more,* she realized with an odd sense of desperation.

"That's it, then," he said, back on his own side of the bed. "One kiss. Good night, Hannah."

If he expected her to respond with a flippant "See you in the morning" he was clearly out of his mind. Kisses like that simply didn't happen every day. Not in her life.

She did a mental inventory of her resources, searching for some semblance of sophistication, or even a small redeeming touch of bravado that would make her appear less than a fool to have kissed him at all.

She smiled up at the ceiling.

"I feel sorry for Adele."

"How's that?" His frown was almost audible.

"That slip she was wearing? You might try buying her something a little nicer if you want to get back in her good graces. It doesn't do a thing for her image to be wearing a blue-light special."

With a smug sense of satisfaction, Hannah rolled over and promptly went to sleep.

This time it was the phone that jarred her awake.

5

GROGGY, Holt lunged across the bed to silence the intrusive instrument. His body collided with a soft, feminine form as his hand—jarred slightly off course—found a hotel pen on the bedside table and sent it spinning to the floor along with a pad of paper. He managed to get one eye marginally open but the phone rang again before he could pick it up. Meanwhile, with Hannah looking up at him with wide-eyed surprise, his morning erection tightened in his groin and pressed purposefully against her thigh.

Hell, it wasn't just the time of day that had him hard.

He'd been sleeping, if you could call it that, all night with a foot-long two-by-four between his legs. He never should have kissed her. Not even once.

Trying to ignore his discomfort, he snatched the phone off the hook just as it rang a third time.

The Corset Queen hammered the wall next door. Damn, she had to be the lightest sleeper in the world. "We're gonna have to get that woman earplugs," he grumbled, entirely forgetting the prearranged Janson-Jansen telephone etiquette. "H'lo."

After a brief pause, Adele's sultry voice said, "I assume that first comment wasn't meant for me."

Both of Holt's eyes popped wide open. "No. Not a chance, babe."

"I also trust I'm not taking you away from anything important."

"Important?" he echoed. Intriguing was a better description. Tempting, too, with the Hannah's sweet, lithe body half-mashed beneath his. It took little imagination to see himself kissing her porcelain skin, starting with her bare shoulders and working his way south. That got him remembering the light suntan line he'd noted that arched across her hips, the shape of her legs and how he'd like to have those same legs wrapped around his waist.

"Holt? Are you still there?"

"Yeah, sure. It's just that we...I mean, I wasn't up yet."

There was weighty pause on the other end of the line. "I see."

Guilt mobilized Holt. He shifted to a safer, less intimate position, and Hannah managed to scramble out from beneath him. She squirmed under the phone cord; her nightgown rucked up to the top of her thighs. Impossibly, lust coiled even more tightly in Holt's gut.

His throat nearly clamped shut. He asked hoarsely, "What is it you wanted, doll?"

From the closet, Hannah snared a dress and a

handful of lingerie. Her nightgown was even more see-through than Holt had remembered.

"I've arranged for you to see Algernon Meat-cleaver this morning. He's the CEO of First Federal and an old friend of mine. He's interested in the aphrodisiac trade. He may want to invest in your project."

"Hey, that's great, Adele. How'd you get a hold of him so early in the morning?"

There was another pregnant pause.

Hannah slipped into the bathroom and closed the door behind her. Holt exhaled.

He couldn't quite recall what question he'd asked Adele when she responded, "Will nine o'clock in your hotel lobby be all right? I'll make the introductions, then I've got to go. I have a nine-thirty appointment with a client at my office."

He shot a glance at the clock. "Perfect. I'll be downstairs. Say, I really appreciate your help, Adele. Particularly after the mix-up last night."

"Don't give it another thought, darling. And give my regards to Miss Jansen."

The phone clicked dead. Holt frowned. How *had* she reached this Meatcleaver guy so early in the morning? he wondered.

But the sound of running water in the bathroom distracted him from pursuing that particular thought. Instead, he got a very clear picture of warm water sluicing over Hannah's shoulders and down her breasts, beading her nipples...

"Ah, hell!" For his own sanity, he had to stop thinking about his roommate that way.

HOLT PUNCHED the Down button for the elevator.

"Here, let me get your sample case," he told Hannah. She was dressed in a sheath dress with a floral jacket that managed, impossibly, to make her eyes even more blue than usual. Her hair was pulled back again, and his fingers itched to strip away the pins that held it in place so he could see her with the blond strands softly brushing her shoulders— just the way she'd looked standing buck-naked in the shower last night.

"I can manage."

His lips quirked. "Yeah, but I'm meeting somebody important downstairs, and I'd just as soon you and Hannah's Frills didn't make one of your famous scenes again."

Laughing, she shook her head. A few strands of blond hair came lose and fluttered against the column of her neck, right at that spot Holt wanted to kiss. "I doubt it would work as well the second time."

The elevator came and they rode down in companionable silence. Holt felt a little more relaxed now that they were away from the natural intimacy of a shared hotel room. He was under control. Sort of. At lunch he'd make arrangements to see Adele again this evening—maybe at her place. Meanwhile, with her connections, he'd line up the loan he needed.

Everything was gonna be just fine.

Then he could go back to his ranch and sit on his porch staring out at the sunset...alone, he realized with a niggling sense of dread.

When the doors opened to the lobby, he gingerly pulled Hannah's case across the elevator threshold. No bumps. No jarring. And certainly no kick to the latch.

In addition to an assortment of business people crowding the lobby, a clutch of YMCA summer day-campers on a field trip had turned the place into a playground for hide-and-seek. Behind every potted plant there was a wannabe juvenile delinquent wearing a sunflower-yellow T-shirt and a bright red scarf tied around his or her nose. The kid who was apparently ''it''—a skinny youngster of about ten with hundred-power magnifying lenses for glasses—was leaning against a marble post, counting. The leaders of Camp Runamok appeared to be among the missing. Perhaps wisely, Holt suspected.

He spotted Adele coming in the front door with a distinguished older guy in a gray suit and matching vest. His crown of white hair was as impeccably styled as Adele's.

''Hang on a minute, Holt.'' Hannah touched his arm. ''There's a man I wanted to see before I set up again for the show. It'll just take me a sec.''

''Go ahead. I see Adele. You can catch up with

me over there.'' He gestured to the far side of the lobby.

With a nod, Hannah headed off in a different direction, her cute little tush swaying with each step.

Holt dragged his gaze away. Man, those jerks in Minnesota must be as blind as the kid playing hide-and-seek.

He started across the lobby. The ''it'' kid looked up, glanced around and began to run—straight into Hannah's sample case, which Holt was dragging behind him. With a whoosh, the kid tumbled over it, smacking onto the marble floor.

Immediately, Holt stooped to check on the youngster.

''You okay?'' he asked.

With amazing resilience, the kid bounced back up, apparently unharmed. He shoved his glasses back into place. ''I'm sorry, mister. I didn't see your suitcase.''

''Maybe running isn't such a good idea when it's so crowded.''

The kid lifted his skinny shoulders in a shrug. ''You see any other kids around? I gotta tag 'em before they get home free or else I'll be 'it' again. I don't see real good.''

''Right.'' Holt didn't entirely want to give the game away but this was one half-pint who needed help. ''Can you find the potted plants?''

The boy squinted and looked around. "Yeah. They're green."

"Try looking behind those."

"Hey, thanks, mister." He was off again at a dead run, kamikaze style.

Keeping alert for any more unguided missiles, Holt crossed the lobby. When he met Adele's gaze, he saw amusement in her eyes.

"Good morning, Holt," she said smoothly. "I'd like you to meet Algie...Algernon Meatcleaver."

Algie? The name sounded like some kind of green slime. "How do you do, sir." Smiling his most winning smile, Holt extended his hand.

While they clasped hands, the banker's gaze slid past Holt and his wrinkle-free forehead pleated ever so slightly. "You neglected to mention, my dear Adele, that your friend is a cross-dresser."

It took a couple of heartbeats before Algie's comment sank in. Adele's lips compressed as she held back a smile. Her dark eyes sparkled with ill-contained mirth.

Puzzled, Holt turned back to look the way he had come. Then he saw the trail of Hannah's Frills he'd left the full width of the lobby and the children scurrying to pick up each fascinating item of underwear.

Meanwhile, the hotel manager was striding toward him. A slender, elegant man with a straight line of a mustache about two whiskers wide, he glared offended daggers at Holt.

"Really, sir," the manager said with all the disdain an aristocratic butler would muster when faced with a vagrant at the back door. "We must ask you to refrain from displaying your merchandise—"

"It's not *my* merchandise."

Adele smiled placidly. "It is tasteful, though. Don't you agree, Algie?"

The manager continued, unmoved with Holt's denial. "As for those naughty children, you really must—"

"They're not my kids, either. And this hotel is so damn stuffy, it's little wonder they're getting bored." And he was getting more frustrated by the minute.

The manager puffed out his chest. For a moment, Holt was afraid he'd gone too far. Getting tossed out of a hotel on his ear had not been a part of his plan.

So much for his insistence that *he* be the one in charge of Hannah's sample case this morning!

Damn! No question, that woman was going to be the death of him. On the other hand, he might just throttle her first and be done with all this anarchy in his life.

A cross-dresser! He'd have this Algie person in court for slander, too.

"So HOW DID Algie react to your proposal this morning?" Adele asked. She and Holt had ordered their lunch and were sipping their glasses of wine.

The restaurant was dark and intimate, their table very private.

"He was okay on the idea, though he didn't seem to have much interest in buffalo meat. He really zeroed in on the aphrodisiac stuff, though. I gave him a copy of my business plan, and he said he'd get back to me."

"That's good."

"Particularly since I'd made such a damn fool of myself with Hannah's Frills. She's a dynamite lady and really determined to succeed, if a bit naive. But she's got some weird ideas about marketing her stuff. Algie was very understanding."

Adele fingered her wineglass thoughtfully. "Yes, he is."

"Of course, Hannah's designs are going to sell themselves eventually. I mean, they are so damn sexy—"

"Which you know from personal experience?"

He frowned. "She showed me her samples, that's all." That wasn't entirely true, since he'd sure as hell seen her wearing her own nightgown design, but the small lie was honest enough for Adele's consumption. "Look, babe, I can't tell you how sorry I am that I blew it the past couple of nights. But that's all over now. I figure we can get together tonight, maybe at your place? We can do dinner in and then—"

The waiter showed up with their salads.

Holt waited while the young man offered a

chilled fork to each of them, and ground pepper on both salads. Then he refilled the wineglasses from the bottle in the bucket of ice. Finally, with an "Enjoy your salads" he discreetly departed to see to the comfort and care of his other patrons.

"Like I said, tonight we can—"

"I'm not sure that's a good idea, Holt."

"Hey, you don't have to worry about Hannah, if that's what's troubling you. I mean this whole mix-up about being roommates is ridiculous. It was only that our names are so close, you know."

"You seem very fond of her."

"Me? Nah, it's just she's a real interesting person. Who would have guessed a woman from a small town in northern Minnesota would have such talent for lingerie design? And she's smart, too. In spite of that innocent air." He forked a bite of chilled lettuce into his mouth. "She really hasn't been around much. Helps her old man run a hardware store, of all things. Does the books, or something, and teaches the local hausfraus how to repair their plumbing. Anybody would want to get away from that."

"Possibly."

Holt got a seriously uncomfortable feeling about what Adele was thinking. "Look, if there's something going on here I need to know about..."

She rested her fork on the edge of the plate. "I guess I'm not being very fair to you."

"Fair?" He studied her sharply. "God, don't tell me it's Algie." Mr. Slick-Green-Slime himself?

"He and I have gotten, well, close in the last few months."

"He's too old for you, Adele. Ancient."

"I prefer to think, in contrast with your innocent Hannah—"

"She's not *my* innocent anything."

"That Algie is a very sophisticated man. And he's extremely wealthy."

"Married?"

She sent him a scathing look. "He's been a widower for some years now. His children are grown."

"Do you love him?"

"I believe, possibly, I do."

Holt felt like he'd swallowed an entire head of lettuce and it was stuck in his craw. "Has he proposed?"

"Yes, several times. I've been putting off my answer, however. It's so hard to be sure what I should do."

Her swift kick to his masculine ego raised his temper a notch. "If you're thinking about getting married, then what the hell did you come up to my room for last night? Was it some kind of a test?"

Eyes lowered, she studied her salad at some length, sorting the various exotic green leaves into separate, matching piles with the tines of her fork. "I'm not exactly proud of myself for trying to use you that way."

"Jeez." With a full range of swearwords on the tip of his tongue, he leaned back in the plush velvet chair. "It figures. Getting it on once a year wasn't enough for a hot lady like you." Nor had it been enough for Holt, either, but he'd had few other choices.

"Don't be crass, darling. It doesn't become you." She sipped her wine again. "If it's any consolation, you're the best lover I've ever had."

"Terrific. Does that mean ol' Algie wants free samples of the aphrodisiacs he's planning to underwrite?"

Lifting her chin, she nailed him with another censorious look. "Algie is a fine, good man, and there is more to life than simply sex. In case you hadn't noticed."

"So you're going to marry him."

"Yes, I am."

"You told me falling into the marriage trap once was enough for you. Just like me."

"A woman always retains the right to change her mind." She rested her hand on his forearm. "Given how taken you are with Hannah, you might want to reevaluate your position, too."

No, he wasn't going to do that. He wasn't going to risk his ranch again; he wasn't going to get himself a wife who'd turn into a lonely, nagging shrew and be unfaithful to boot.

No, he had no plans to get married a second time.

A man who doesn't learn the lessons life tosses in his direction is the worst kind of fool.

HANNAH STRAIGHTENED the Hannah's Frills banner she'd hung at the back of her display booth and sighed. The afternoon had been impossibly slow. Hardly anyone had stopped by to examine her designs.

"Hey, don't look so grim. Business will pick up tomorrow. The out-of-towners from the west coast and the South will begin arriving tonight."

She turned to Sam Spivak in the adjacent booth. "You think so?"

"Absolutely." Arms folded, he rested against the edge of his display table. "It always works that way. Second day of the show drags by like molasses and then things get crazy over the weekend."

That would be good because, with little to do, Hannah was thinking about Holt far too much. Wondering how his meeting with the banker had gone that morning, particularly given the repeat performance of her lingerie being strung out clear across the lobby. She kept thinking about his lunch with Adele—where they'd eat and, more annoyingly, what they might do after they'd eaten.

It wasn't healthy for a woman to give so much thought to a man's relationship with another woman. Like a persistent horde of wood ticks, unwanted jealousy bored under her skin and festered there.

From the pocket of his garish plaid sports jacket, Sam pulled out his harmonica—his "shtick" as he called it—to lure a crowd to his booth when things got slow.

"How 'bout I cheer you up with a little ditty or two? Got any favorites?"

"Just don't play anything too romantic," she told him with a wry smile. "I'm not in the mood." Actually, she *was* very much in the mood, which was exactly the problem.

He cocked an eyebrow. "Hey, kiddo, you missing some boyfriend you left back home?"

"No, there's no one back home." There never had been. "It's my...roommate."

"Roommate? Honey, if there's something really bothering you, you can tell ol' Sammy Spivak. I can be a real good listener."

Because Sam was such a basically nice guy, and Hannah needed someone to talk to, she did tell him. About how she and Holt had become roommates. The odd feelings she got whenever he was around. How much he loved his ranch. And his friend, Adele.

About the only thing she omitted was the kiss she had shared with Holt and how they slept together in the same bed. That seemed a little too personal, and besides, her response had been far too unsettling to tell anyone.

"Looks to me, kiddo, like you're coming down with a bad case of lovesickness," he said when she finished the tale. "Gotta be careful about that kind of stuff when you're a long way from home."

"Yes, I suppose you're right."

"'Course, it could be the real thing, I suppose. Can't tell for sure unless you take it a step or two further."

Heat raced to her cheeks as she imagined what those "steps" would entail. "I couldn't do that."

"He's a decent enough guy, isn't he?"

"Well, yes, but he has a girlfriend."

"That would slow down a respectable lady like you a bit, I imagine."

"It certainly would." She giggled nervously. "Besides, Bubbles Von Hemmelrich is in the room next door to us. Any little noise we make, she starts pounding on the wall. I can imagine the ruckus she'd make if we, I mean, we'd have to be quiet as two little mice."

Sam threw back his head and his booming laughter bounced around the room. "Tell you what, kiddo. If you decide to get it on with this roommate of yours, I'll get one of the guys to take Bubbles to the bar. Her Achilles' heel is something the bartender calls a Rocky Mountain Mud Slide. I think it's a chocolate-brandy milk shake. Potent stuff, they tell me. A couple of those little puppies under her belt, and the Queen will sleep like a baby princess."

"I'll keep that in mind." Though Hannah doubted she'd have much use for the information.

About that time, a man strolled up the aisle and stopped at Hannah's booth. He was younger than most of the buyers, under forty, well-dressed in a suit and tie, and would have been handsome except his nose was a little bulbous.

"You're new to the show this year, aren't you?" he asked.

"Yes, but I've been designing lingerie for several years and perfecting the fit and comfort of my garments," she told him.

He picked up a side-zip minigirdle made of floral nylon and spandex, and turned it inside out, inspecting the seams with authority. He tested the strength and resilience of the fabric by tugging.

"I pride myself on designing garments that are just as comfortable for a woman who is a size sixteen as for someone who wears a three."

"Yes, very nice." He righted the girdle and placed it back on the table. "I'll be here a few more days. Perhaps I'll drop by again." He handed her a business card and left, walking slowly down the aisle examining the other displays.

When Hannah looked at the card, she felt a flutter of excitement. Jonas Zimmermann was vice president of an exclusive chain of women's shops with outlets all through the midwest, a retail success story founded by his father.

Her head snapped up to follow his path as he moved through the hall, and she smiled. Until now, Zimmer's Fine Ladies' Wear had always featured lingerie designed by Bubbles Von Hemmelrich and her minions.

Now wouldn't *that* be a coup!

MOST OF THE DISPLAY booths closed up early that evening due to the lack of customers. After Hannah had tucked her samples in her case again, she went with Sam and his buddies to have a drink just as she had done the previous evening. They tried to joke her into ordering a Mud Slide, but she wisely stuck with a soft drink. Given the very strong suspicion that she was falling head over heels for her roommate, she needed to keep her wits about her.

It was early when she went upstairs, about seven o'clock, and she was thinking about ordering room service for dinner. She hadn't had any message from Holt to steer clear of the room. Even so, she stood in front of the door for several long heartbeats, listening hard to see if there was anyone inside.

In an effort to minimize any possible embarrassment, she knocked before sliding her key card into the slot. She opened the door cautiously and stepped inside. Holt's jeans were tossed carelessly on the bed, his boots were on the floor, and he was just coming out of the bathroom, his hair damp from a shower.

Hannah's breath lodged in her throat and, in spite of all her good intentions to remain sophisticated and aloof, her eyes widened. Thank *goodness* he had one of those big, fluffy towels wrapped around his waist.

"I'll just wait outside till you're—" Her voice squeaked.

"Hang on." Casual about his near nakedness, he scooped up his clothes from the bed. "It'll just take me a minute to get decent."

Hannah did a precise, military-style about-face that would have made her brother proud and stared at the close door. However, the image of Holt's broad shoulders, muscular chest and powerful cowboy legs covered with springy dark hair remained vivid in her mind.

"Guess you're getting ready to go out with Adele," she said after drawing a steadying breath. Blinking furiously, she tried to drive his image away. And failed miserably.

"Nope. We're not going out."

"Oh. Then I guess you'll want me out of here so you two can—"

"She's getting married."

Hannah whirled, shocked. "You're going to marry her?"

"Not me." He slid his arms into a silver-blue Western-cut shirt but didn't bother to button it up. He hadn't buttoned his jeans, either. "Some banker who's as old as the hills and has megabucks."

Hannah tried to suppress a surge of relief. Or maybe it was elation. "I'm sorry."

"Don't be. She says she loves the guy."

She hooked her hand through the handle of her sample case and dragged it across the room to the closet. "I feel like this is all my fault. I mean, if I hadn't messed up your plans—"

"She's been seeing him for a while. You're not to blame. Nobody is. Stuff happens. People change."

Even though Holt didn't seem all that upset about his broken relationship with Adele, Hannah still felt guilty.

Holt had been very nice about this entire roommate mix-up. It seemed like there ought to be something she could do to make amends for whatever amount of fault was hers. After all, he'd come all this way to Chicago to see Adele and he'd been counting on—

Well, he'd also needed a bank loan.

Which he still might land, she supposed.

But he'd missed out on—

Usually Hannah didn't act on impulse. She was methodical when she handled the hardware store's books, and worked with craftsmanlike care when she created her lingerie designs. But sometimes a woman simply had to take advantage of what opportunities came her way.

Particularly if, in doing so, she could make up for a small inconvenience she'd caused another person. A person she cared about.

She looked up at Holt and smiled a little shakily.

"Say, I have this small problem, and I wondered if you could maybe help me out with it."

He picked up a pocket comb from the desk and ran it through his damp hair, smoothing the thick waves. "Sure, if I can."

"You see, I'm probably the oldest virgin in Crookston. Maybe even in all of Minnesota."

"Hannah!" His brows lowered into a stern frown. "What the hell are you talking about?"

"Well..." She licked her lips, determined to go on in spite of the way he was glowering at her. "I thought maybe, since Adele's not in the picture anymore, and assuming you're not doing anything special tonight, you could rectify that little problem for me."

6

"No!" Holt exploded.

Hannah took a step back and her breasts rose on a quick intake of air.

Lowering his voice, Holt tried to rein in his reaction. "Are you crazy?" Or maybe he was the one who'd lost his mind, because her request seemed so damn reasonable. And tempting. To even consider agreeing to her request to relieve her of her virginity went well beyond the bounds of sanity. And yet...

"But you said I was sexy." Her chin trembled ever so slightly as she lifted it to a stubborn angle.

Holt cursed himself for being so damn tactless. He hadn't meant to hurt her. The offer was more than he'd ever expected to hear and he felt honored. But accepting her invitation would rank him right up there with people who bungee-jump off the Grand Coulee Dam.

"Being sexy has got nothing to do with anything. You simply can't go around asking men to *fix* that kind of a problem. Not that it's a problem at all. It's actually admirable. But someone's likely to take you up on the idea of, well, deflowering you."

"Is that such a horrible thought? I mean, doing it with me?"

Jamming his comb into his hip pocket, he paced to the far side of the room. When he turned, he realized he couldn't put nearly enough distance between them to reduce the captivating impulse he felt to do just what she desired.

"Of course not. It's just that—" *That what?* he wondered, his fists clenched, a muscle ticking in his jaw. That he'd been thinking about little else but getting into her panties for the past two days? Is that what he was upset about, the reason his teeth were on edge, and other parts of his anatomy rigid in anticipation? "It's just that a man doesn't like to be used for a one-night stand any more than a woman does."

"You were going to sleep with Adele for a night or two and then go back home," she pointed out reasonably, in spite of a little quiver of her lower lip. "Why is sleeping with me any different?"

"Because you *are* a virgin, damn it!" He stalked back toward her. Another mistake, he realized, inhaling her wildflower scent. "The first time, well... It's supposed to be special for you, with someone you care about."

"Was it special for you?" she asked in a voice so low and intimate it was like a soft summer rain slipping over his skin on a blistering hot day.

Her question brought him up short for a second.

"That's different. I'm a man. Men's hormones can make them do really stupid things."

Her gaze slid to the bed behind him. "Women have hormones, too. Lots of them."

"Yeah, well." He swallowed hard. *No,* this was one time when he was *not* going to succumb, raging hormones or not. "Come on, Hannah, you know you're not the kind of girl who hops into the sack with any ol' guy she happens to meet in a hotel room."

"I *don't* know that. It's never happened before. That I've stayed in a hotel room with a man, I mean. Before you."

He narrowed his eyes. "You'd regret it in the morning."

She never even flinched. "I regret I haven't found anyone I wanted to do *it* with. It seems to me one kind of regret is just as bad as another."

The woman must have taken an advanced course in logic. She was thinking too fast for him. And Holt's resolve was weakening by the minute. In order to survive, he'd have to go on the offensive.

"Listen to me, Hannah. I've been around a lot more than you have and know how women react to these things." Though, admittedly, he'd grown a little rusty on the subject these last few years. "Let's say we got it on together real good. You know, rockets and fireworks, that kind of thing. It's a new experience for you. The first time. You'd make more of it than simply good sex. You'd start thinking about living together, commitment, maybe even having a family together.''

She shook her head in denial. Strands of hair had apparently been coming lose from her bun all day, and now formed a veil of blond softness at the back of her neck. ''I'd never say a word about marriage. I promise. I'm only saying we'd do it once. It doesn't seem to me that would be such a terrible imposition.''

''That's exactly what I mean, sweetheart. I'm talking about maybe living together—just as an example, you understand—and the first word that pops out of your mouth is marriage. We come from two different worlds, honey. And matrimony isn't a part of my vocabulary.''

''I see.'' She did a courageous job of raising her chin again, a show of bravado he had to admire. Accepting rejection gracefully took a whole lot of guts.

Lightly, she said, ''Well, no harm done by asking, I always say.''

If he hadn't seen the glitter in her eyes before Hannah turned away, Holt might have thought he'd let her down gently. But the sudden glistening of tears was a dead giveaway. He'd hurt her.

He couldn't leave her hanging there, thinking she wasn't attractive. Or that he didn't want to be seen with her. *Or go to bed with her so much it hurt.*

For that reason, more than anything else, he didn't dare be alone with Hannah. Not now. Not when he was teetering on the edge of forgetting all the lessons life had taught him about men and women, and relationships, and how they fell apart when the going got tough. And how he wouldn't want to put a woman like Hannah through the kind of marital mess that he had endured.

"Say, have you ever been to a baseball game?" he asked.

Hannah had to force herself to swallow several times before her throat cleared enough that she was able to answer Holt's unexpected question. "Crookston's Little League team made it to the state finals one year. Some of my friends had children playing and I went to the games."

"Great. The Chicago Cubs are playing tonight. Wrigley Field. The team's awful, as usual, but seeing a major-league game is a real experience. Something we don't see much of in Montana. Wanna give it a try? Unless you have other plans," he added.

She pursed her lips. He was doing something kind, trying to make amends. She knew that, and wished she could feel more grateful. "No, I don't have other plans." Not since he'd turned down the one activity she thought they might both enjoy. Obviously, she'd been wrong and had totally overestimated her ability to attract someone of the opposite sex. Particularly a man of substantial experience.

"Terrific. We'll sit in the outfield bleachers, hiss

and boo at the other team, and have dinner there. Hot dogs. Beer. The whole enchilada. How does that sound?''

Very much like second best. But Hannah didn't want to admit that.

So she turned from groping blindly in her suitcase for a change of clothes and gave Holt her most brilliant smile. "You're right. Baseball sounds like a lot more fun than what I had in mind.''

THEY TOOK A CAB to the stadium and arrived during the top of the second inning. The score was already three to zero for the visiting team, but everyone said the Cubs were just getting warmed up.

Holt had indeed been right about a major-league game being fun, Hannah decided. The fans were raucous, jeering their own team as much as the opposition. Hannah learned to do the wave with the crowd, and managed to get her hands on a beach ball, sending it sailing on across the stands, recreational activities that appeared designed to keep baseball fans occupied during deadly-dull innings when nothing much else was happening.

The hot dogs were cold, the beer mostly warm, the peanuts salty.

She loved it because she loved being with Holt. His sexy smile flashed in her direction more than once; his arm looped around her shoulders, protecting her from rowdy fans, who were bent on shoving everyone else out of the bleachers. Unintentionally, she assumed, due to their high good spirits.

When the Cubs managed to lose by a single run after ten innings, and Holt escorted her back to the hotel on the crowded El, Hannah cherished the feel of being mashed against his big, brawny body. His shirt smelled of the outdoors, mustard and clean, masculine sweat.

At the hotel, they rode up the elevator in silence, their fingers entwined, Hannah just a little breathless with the quick change of elevation. Or maybe because of Holt's closeness.

He used his key card and shoved open the door.

"Look, Hannah, there's something I need to do. Go ahead and get ready for bed. I'll be back, ah, later."

She could hardly argue with the man. If he wanted to be somewhere else now, that was his business. The fact that her whole body was thrumming with the need for a greater intimacy was not his problem.

"Sure," she said bravely. "Just be quiet when you come in. I'm beat."

He leaned forward as though he might want to kiss her good-night. But then he turned away and walked down the hall toward the elevators, leaving Hannah feeling as though an icy Minnesota blizzard had just whipped down the corridor.

In spite of her disappointment, she dressed for bed and crawled between the sheets, leaving the bathroom light on and the door open a crack so he wouldn't stumble in the dark. Eventually she drifted off to sleep. Sometime in the early hours, she rolled over. The clock said four. Holt had still not returned to their room.

She mashed her eyes closed again and tried not to acknowledge the trickle of tears that were edging down her cheeks.

When she woke in the morning—this time without the aid of an alarm clock or clamoring phone—Holt's side of the bed remained empty.

Anxiety snatched her breath away. Maybe Holt had gone for a walk after he'd left her and had been mugged on the mean streets of the city. Even now he might be lying in some dirty alleyway, bleeding, alone and unnoticed. And she hadn't reported him missing when he hadn't returned to the room as he said he would. She hadn't gone in search of him.

In the next heartbeat, she realized a more likely scenario was that Adele had changed her mind. They were probably together. Unbelievably, that thought hurt even more than thinking Holt had been mugged, and a low moan escaped her lips.

"Get real," she told herself. "Holt's a big boy and can certainly take care of himself. And he doesn't have to check in with you."

Sternly pulling herself together, she showered and dressed. That done, she still had a few minutes to spare before she had to go downstairs and, feeling restless, she decided to call her father.

"Hope you'll get on home soon, Hannie, girl," he said almost without preamble. "We got a letter from the IRS yesterday."

"What about?"

"I don't know. I left it for you."

"Well, don't worry. It's probably forms for our quarterly returns." Though it would have been easy enough for him to have opened the envelope. "Are you managing the daily receipts all right?"

"Saved the register tape for you and stuffed the cash in the back of the drawer for when you get back."

"But Dad, it'll be the weekend when I get home. We'll have to wait till Monday to deposit the cash."

"Won't hurt this one time."

But it would mean extra work for Hannah. "Did you finish the leftover roast beef I saved for you?"

"Nope."

She frowned. "Why not?" She'd carefully planned easy-to-fix meals for the few days she'd be away. All he'd had to do was zap individual packets in the microwave. "You have to eat properly."

"I am. First night you were gone, Margaret Clausen brought me over a batch of fried chicken and some of her dumplings."

"Oh. That was very nice of her."

"And last night she came by with a casserole and a fresh peach pie."

Her brows rose. It seems the neighbor lady, a woman who'd been widowed even longer than her father had, had taken a sudden interest in Terence Jansen. Or maybe Margaret had simply been biding her time until Hannah was out from underfoot.

"Well, it sounds like you're getting along just fine," she told her father.

"Yep. Miss you, though. Be glad to have you back home."

Hannah said, "I'll be glad, too," but the words nearly stuck in her throat. The thought of the claustrophobic back room of the hardware store choked her; that, combined with her memory of the odors of ink and oil and dust and metal shavings suddenly made her nauseous.

"Look, Dad, I've gotta go set up my display. Love you a lot."

"Me, too, Hannie, girl."

She did love her father. But here in Chicago she'd caught a glimpse of something else she wanted even more than escape from her life in Crookstown; she wanted a big, handsome cowboy from out west.

At the moment, however, the chances of her landing that dream seemed even more remote than the possibility of finding buyers for her lingerie designs.

HOLT RAN his palm over his morning stubble. No man should have to sleep in a chair all night, not even a comfortable one in a posh hotel lobby. The night manager had rousted him once. But the display of his room key, a quick check of his registration, and the slightest hint that Holt was having some small disagreement with the woman with whom he was sharing the room elicited considerable sympathy.

"Women are an unpredictable lot, sir," the manager had said solemnly. "I quite understand your situation, and I assure you, you are not the first gentleman to experience a woman's scorn in this hotel."

Holt had thanked him for his understanding with more enthusiasm than he felt, and settled back into the green-plush chair in a secluded, quiet corner of the lobby. At one point during the night, the smooth, waxy leaves of the potted plant had brushed against his cheek. Holt had been so damn sure it was Hannah caressing him with her fingertips that he'd sat up with a start.

The dream had taken far longer to shake off than the broad leaf he'd yanked in frustration from the plant.

The only other alternative to sleeping in the lobby had been to go back upstairs. To Hannah. And to that big bed they shared.

This time he knew damn well he wouldn't be able to restrain himself. There would have been nothing to separate them, not even a thin layer of crisp, white sheet. And sure as hell not that sheer nightgown she wore.

He shoved his feet back into his boots, stood, rotated his shoulders, then finger-combed his hair.

He sighed, recalling how great Hannah had been at the ball game last night. Maybe she hadn't realized every guy within twenty seats of them had been hot for her. When she'd laughed at some stupid antic on the field or in the bleachers—a wonderful sound that made him think of fast-flowing water tumbling over a bed of rocks in a high-mountain stream—every man around reacted in the same way. They wanted her.

So did Holt.

And he couldn't have her.

A decent man didn't take a woman's virginity, say "Thank you very much," then jet on home to Montana. Even a cynical cowboy like Holt lived by a code that didn't permit such callous behavior.

Whatever she was offering.

He looked around the lobby. There should be a barbershop somewhere nearby. A hot towel, a few strokes with a sharp razor and some fiery aftershave ought to wake him up.

Assuming the barber didn't slit his throat for being stupid enough to turn down Hannah's sweet, sexy offer.

HOLT AVOIDED their room until he was certain Hannah would have left for the lingerie show, then he went upstairs to change.

Feeling at loose ends, he returned to the lobby

about midmorning. He was giving some thought to calling Adele's banker friend when he spotted Hannah entering the elevator with a man—a tall, skinny guy wearing a suit with double-width shoulder pads and a power tie. A good-looking guy with a fresh hair cut.

The way the two of them were talking so amenably grated on Holt's nerves. He didn't like the suit's quick, flashing smile. Or the way his hand slid possessively to Hannah's waist as they entered the elevator.

"Damn!" Holt knew full well what she was up to.

He'd turned down her little scheme to help her get rid of her virginity. Now she'd found someone else to take care of the problem.

Well, he'd have none of it!

As he watched with growing dismay, the elevator rose to the twentieth floor and stopped.

He wasn't going to let her ruin her entire life on a foolish fling with some man she'd just met.

That simply wasn't going to happen, not while she was *his* roommate.

A man had to take responsibility for someone as trusting and innocent as Hannah. Holt was confident that given some time to think about the mistake she was about to make, she would come to her senses.

In a few quick strides, Holt crossed the lobby to

the house phones. He punched the number for room service.

"I'm in the lobby right now and on my way up to my room. I'd like to have a..." He thought furiously, more interested in interrupting what was going on in the room rather than providing sustenance. "A big pot of coffee and a club sandwich."

"Yes, sir. Your name and room number, sir?"

Holt gave him the information.

"It will be about twenty minutes, sir."

He frowned. A lot could happen between a man and a woman in twenty minutes. "Make it under fifteen and there'll be a big tip for you."

"Yes, sir!" Holt could hear the eagerness in the waiter's voice.

7

HANNAH HAD BARELY settled down to show Jonas Zimmermann her portfolio of bridal peignoir and teddy designs, which she hadn't yet made into samples, when there was a knock on the door.

Assuming it was Holt seeking access to the room, her heart kicked in with an extra beat.

Standing, she said, "Excuse me, Mr. Zimmermann. I'll just see who's there."

"Of course. I'll browse through your sketches, if I may."

"Please do."

At the door, she peered through the peephole. To her dismay it wasn't Holt at all but a stranger. "Who is it?" she asked.

"Room service, ma'am." He adjusted his position so she could see the covered tray he was carrying and the hotel name-badge he was wearing.

"We didn't order anything."

"Mr. Janson did, ma'am. He said it was a rush." The eager young man, his face distorted by the fish-eye lens of the peephole, smile broadly at her.

"Oh?" She glanced over her shoulder at Zimmermann, who was occupied with her portfolio.

Perhaps Holt was on his way up to the room now, which might be a little inconvenient with a prospective client on hand, but she supposed they could talk their way around any awkwardness. "Very well."

She opened the door. With a nod and another friendly smile, the waiter walked in. He placed the tray on the desk near the window, then turned and handed her the chit to sign.

She did and said, "Thank you."

The young man continued to gaze at her expectantly. "It was only twelve minutes, ma'am."

"Twelve minutes?"

"Yes, ma'am. Since Mr. Janson called."

"I see. Well, that's very efficient service, I'm sure."

"Here at the Towers, ma'am, we pride ourselves on our speedy service."

"Of course. Thank you again."

He didn't budge. It was as if his feet had been nailed to the floor.

Hannah pulled herself up to her full five feet four inches and straightened her spine. If he was looking for a tip, he could just keep on looking. She wasn't as much of a country bumpkin as he might think. She'd read the charge slip. It clearly indicated a fifteen-percent gratuity was already included.

"Here you are, young man." To Hannah's dismay and total mortification, Jonas Zimmermann handed the waiter a couple of dollar bills.

The waiter looked at the money, lifted his nose with an almost audible sniff, and departed without so much as a thank-you. What amazing arrogance!

"You shouldn't have done that, Mr. Zimmermann. The tip was included in the bill—"

"Apparently he wanted a little something extra."

She reached for her purse. "I'm so embarrassed. Here, let me pay you back."

"Don't trouble yourself, Ms. Jansen. The opportunity to see your designs is worth considerably more than a mere two-dollar tip. You're a very talented designer." With a pleasant smile, he turned back to the portfolio. "Now tell me about this peignoir. Have you developed any cost estimates for its manufacture?"

Hannah basked in Mr. Zimmermann's praise for the next several minutes, at the same time trying valiantly to remain professional when she really wanted to jump up in the air and click her heels together. He really did like her designs!

But then there was another knock on the door.

"I'm really sorry..." she said, backing away from Mr. Zimmermann as he continued to study a rough sketch of a lace bodysuit she created after listening to a day's worth of Western music on her hometown radio station, courtesy of the apparently near-deaf adolescent who'd been trimming hedges and mowing the lawn next door.

She peeped through the viewing hole at the caller. "Yes?"

"Housekeeping," announced the stout little woman.

"You've already cleaned in here."

"I've got the extra towels you ordered, miss."

Extra towels? Whatever was going on?

She let the maid in, who dutifully delivered an armload of towels to the bathroom that would have been sufficient to last a family of ten at least a month. She appeared in no hurry to depart, however, moving toward the door with all the speed of tree sap in the dead of winter.

Hannah ground her teeth. "Thank you. That will be all for now."

The woman opened her mouth to speak, then wheeled around and finally plodded out the door, pulling it closed behind her with a loud bang.

Hannah exhaled and returned her attention to Mr. Zimmermann. That lasted about two minutes before the phone rang.

"What!" She nearly shouted into the phone.

There was a lengthy pause before a sultry, feminine voice said, "Miss Jansen, this is Adele Plotkins. Is Holt there?"

"No, he's not."

"Oh. I got an urgent message that I should call him. I don't suppose you know where—"

"No, I don't." But Hannah wished she did because she had a sneaky suspicion he was behind converting their room into Grand Central Station. Though why he would do such a ridiculous thing was totally beyond her. "If I see him I'll tell him you called."

There was a knock on the door.

Distractedly, Hannah hung up the phone.

"Perhaps this isn't a good time," Mr. Zimmermann said, almost apologetically. "We can always meet later to discuss—"

"No, this is a fine time. It's just that—"

There was a plumber at the door, a big, burly guy wearing overalls and a overflowing tool belt. "Somebody says your toilet's busted."

"No, it's fine. I fixed it myself. Really—"

But the plumber wasn't listening. He sauntered into the bathroom and started banging and crashing things around with about as much finesse as a gorilla who'd been given a hammer to play with.

Hannah rolled her eyes. Her career was at stake and she'd suddenly acquired an entourage of thousands determined to provide services she didn't want or need, and certainly hadn't ordered.

This couldn't be happening to her!

But it was.

The next caller at the door was the air-conditioning mechanic. To her amazement, he opened the sliding glass door to the balcony, frightening a pair of gulls from their perch, and peered outside. "If you're too cold, just let in some of the good hot air from outside. That'll fix you right up."

The warm breeze caught a few papers on the desk, swirling them to the floor.

"We're trying to have a meeting here," Hannah complained. "Could you do all this later?" Assuming it needed to be done at all.

The mechanic acted as though he hadn't heard a word. He pushed the bed out of the way so he could use a stepladder to get at the vent, which he wrenched open with a horrible screech, the equivalent of a thousand pieces of chalk scraping on a thousand blackboards.

Hannah winced, her teeth set on edge.

The limit of her patience had been reached. And then some!

"I'll be right back, Mr. Zimmermann. Pleased don't let all this—" she gestured vaguely "—disturb you."

Before he could answer, she was out the door. She was going to find Holt Janson, and when she got through with him, he'd think busting broncos was a walk in the park compared to going toe-to-toe with her.

SHE DIDN'T HAVE far to go, though she might have missed him if the slow-as-molasses elevator hadn't taken so long to arrive.

From the corner of her eye she caught a movement, just a flash, leaving an impression of a tall, masculine body topped by a full head of walnut-brown hair. She turned quickly. The only telltale signs that anyone was lingering in the alcove at the end of the hall were the tips of a pair of cowboy boots poking out around the corner.

The jerk! His big feet gave him away.

She stormed down the hall and cornered him. "What in the name of sweet peace do you think you're doing?"

He backed up a step. "I'm saving you from yourself, that's what I'm doing."

"Oh, fried green apples! What do you think you're saving me from? This is my career we're talking about. My future!"

"You deserve better than a one-night stand."

She looked at him blankly.

"That man in there." He gestured toward their room. "How long have you known him?"

"I met him yesterday," she said slowly. "Why?"

"I'd bet my best saddle the guy is in town looking for a good time, some heavy-duty action. He said he's here on business, right?"

"Yes, he is."

"See, what'd I tell you? He's on the make—he's slipped the reins. He's probably got a wife at home and a couple of kids. Maybe more."

"So what does that have to do with anything? I don't care if he's married or not."

He stared at her incredulously. "You don't?"

"Of course not. Ours is strictly a business relationship."

"Business? My God, Hannah, you can't do

this." He took her by the shoulders and dragged her into the alcove, their bodies colliding. "Your virginity isn't something you sell off like a few hundred acres of scrub growth you don't need anymore. It's important."

"My...what?" Her voice cracked.

"Listen to me, sweetheart. Some guy will come along, I promise you. A man who's worth waiting for. You don't want to waste your virginity on—"

She started to giggle. She couldn't help herself. The alternative would be to burst into tears.

"This isn't a laughing matter," he said sternly. His eyebrows drew into a straight line.

"But it is. You see, you thought—" Another paroxysm of laughter seized her.

"Cut it out, Hannah. This is serious business."

"Yes, it is." She sobered instantly. "The man you are so confident is going to wrest my virginity from me is Jonas Zimmermann, vice president of Zimmer's Fine Ladies' Wear, the owner and founder's son. He's looking at my lingerie designs right now—assuming he hasn't lost all interest due to the army of maintenance people who've been swarming all over our room. And assuming he's isn't madder than hops because he had to pop for a two-dollar tip when the waiter wouldn't clear out without a little something extra. All because of you," she accused.

"Ladies' wear?"

"*Upscale* ladies' wear. And if he decides to buy

my designs—and he seems very, very interested—
I'm in fat city, Holt. Hog heaven, as they say in my
part of the country. Then I can walk out of my
father's hardware store when he retires, turn the key
in the lock and never look back."

His jaw dropped. "I didn't know."

"You didn't ask!" she wailed.

His grip on her shoulders eased, and his hands
slid down her back to rest on the swell of her hips.
"I'm sorry, Hannah. I guess I kinda jumped the
gun, didn't I?" His fingers flexed against her soft
flesh.

A sudden tremor passed through her. "Yes, you
did." His hands were too big, too masculine and
sending far too much heat through the fabric of her
skirt.

As though he was aware of her reaction, the dark
circles of his irises expanded.

"Guess I should keep my nose out of your business." His gaze played over her face, raising color
in her cheeks.

"I'd appreciate that." The tension stretched
tightly between them, thick and palpable in the
empty hallway. The elevator motor hummed, the
vibrations more felt than heard through the lush car-
pet and padding. A guest room door opened somewhere, then closed with a solid click.

Blood thrummed through Hannah's veins, gath-
ering warmly near her center. Her breathing grew
shallow. She licked her lips.

His hands moved closer together over her hips, then lower to cup her derriere. The impulse to lean into him was almost beyond enduring. She ached to press her throbbing breasts to his chest. He could ease this longing she felt, she knew he could.

Never before had she been so vulnerable to a man. Or felt so needy.

But he'd rejected her overtures once.

Her pride wouldn't allow him a second chance to refuse her. He had, after all, chosen to sleep somewhere else last night.

Both bemused and frustrated by her own reactions, she placed her palms on his chest and managed to say, "I've got to get back to Mr. Zimmermann."

He held her for a moment more, his expression strained as though he were struggling for control, and then he let her go. "I'll stay out of your way."

"Thank you." The words stuck in her throat like corset boning swallowed crosswise.

At the elevator bank, he pressed the call button. She kept on walking toward their room, head held high in spite of knees that had turned the consistency of aging rubber falsies.

Reaching the door, she placed her hand on the knob. Behind her, the elevator dinged as it arrived on the floor. The doors swished open.

She drew a steadying breath and turned the knob.

"Oh, *parsnips!*" she cried. She'd forgotten her card key when she went out to confront Holt. Now

Mr. Zimmermann, and who knew how many work-men, were inside the room without her. She hated to knock. It would hardly make a good impression on a prospective client if he thought she was so bubbleheaded that she'd left without her key.

Which, of course, was the truth. But she'd had a darn good reason to be distracted.

Whirling, she raced back down the hallway. She reached the elevator just as the doors slid firmly shut. She pounded her fists on the door. "Holt!"

It was no good. He was on his way down twenty floors—to the bowels of the earth as far as reaching him was concerned—and it could take forever for the next elevator to come. Finding him once she got downstairs might be impossible, and would cer-tainly take up more time than she had to waste, particularly since she'd already left Mr. Zimmer-mann alone with her portfolio too long as it was.

She blew out a sigh.

She'd simply have to confess she'd stupidly for-gotten her key.

At the door, she'd raised her hand to knock when the door opened by itself.

The plumber appeared. "It's all taken care of now, ma'am. Call if you need anything else."

From the departing air-conditioning mechanic she heard, "I screwed the vent down tight. It shouldn't bother you no more. Keep the window open for a while till the temperature warms up."

"Thank you," she said to the pair of departing brawny backs.

Zimmermann stepped into the hallway. "I'm quite impressed with your work, Ms. Jansen. I'll be in touch shortly, I assure you."

Smiling faintly, she watched in horror as the door closed and latched behind him. To prevent that from happening she would have had to slam him out of the way with a body block worthy of a Minnesota Vikings' linebacker.

"That's wonderful, Mr. Zimmermann. I'll look forward to your call."

He extended his hand. "Call me Jonas. Please. Whenever someone says *Mr.* Zimmermann, I have a tendency to look over my shoulder to see where Dad is."

As they shook hands, the door to the adjacent room opened.

"Why Jonas, dear boy! I thought I heard your voice." Shooting Hannah a quelling look, Bubbles Von Hemmelrich hooked her arm through Jonas's elbow and propelled him down the hallway. "Isn't it positively dreadful how noisy hotels can be? Workmen at it all day and all night, the walls thin as paper. Now tell me, dear boy, how's your sweet father?"

Leaning her forehead against the closed and locked door to her room, Hannah thought she was very likely going to be sick.

But when she straightened, vowing not to give in to a threatening wave of despair, she noticed Von

Hemmelrich's door was slightly ajar. A bit of fabric, perhaps the hem of a skirt hanging in the closet, had gotten caught in the crack.

The thoughtful thing to do would be to pull the door shut. After all, Hannah would not want even Bubbles's hotel room to be burglarized simply because she had failed to perform a small act of courtesy.

But as she reached for the door, Hannah realized she was too weary and momentarily too discouraged to face going down to the lobby and admitting to the front desk that she'd locked herself out of the room. That would require another trip upstairs, only to have to return to the lobby level again and resume her post at her display booth.

It would be so much easier and faster, she rationalized, if she went in through Von Hemmelrich's room, stepped out onto the balcony—never once looking down—and entered her own room through the sliding glass door the air-conditioning mechanic had left open.

Yes, that was exactly what she would do—for the sake of efficiency.

The first part of her plan went very well.

She trespassed into Bubbles's room with honest intentions; she looked neither left nor right en route to the window, making no effort to sneak a peek at lingerie designs that might give her a leg up on the competition. Besides, she admitted, Bubbles's staff had all their designs on display downstairs.

Taking a deep breath, she opened the sliding

door, stepped outside, and closed the door behind her. Enormously proud of her cleverness, she hiked up her skirt and lifted her leg over the low railing.

That's when Captain Hook and his girlfriend attacked her with a flurry of squawks and a blizzard of feathers.

Only then did she make the mistake of looking down.

HOLT STALKED through the lobby and out the revolving door into the heat of the day. He ought to get on his horse and ride on back to Montana. Algie Meatcleaver could send along his check if he decided to invest in his deer-antler business.

And Holt would be free of Hannah Jansen.

Damn, but he'd made a fool of himself!

How could he have been so stupid as to think she'd pick up some guy—a stranger—and ask him up to their room to—

Well, he didn't want to think about the details of what he'd thought they were doing. He should have known she wasn't that kind of a woman. Still a *virgin!* It might seem like an anachronism in this day and age, but on Hannah it worked.

By damn, the man who landed her would be one lucky son-of-a—

A crowd was gathered on the sidewalk. They all had their heads tipped back, craning up toward the top of the Towers Hotel. Instinctively, Holt did the same.

He squinted. A tiny figure was plastered against

the wall way up there, maybe twenty stories up, on one of the balconies. Just frozen there while a couple of screeching gulls made low, swooping passes like they were dive-bombing the poor sucker.

Yep, it was just about the twentieth floor—

"Hannah!" he shouted, recognition finally slicing through him.

Without waiting for a response, he propelled himself back into the hotel and to the bank of elevators. He jabbed the call button so hard he was lucky the plastic didn't break. When the elevator finally arrived, he all but dragged the occupants out of the car, waved off an elderly couple who wanted to go Up, and hit the Close Door button and held it, praying for an express ride.

His prayer was answered.

As the doors opened on his floor, he sprinted out of the elevator and down the hall. Seconds later he was standing on the balcony next to Hannah. Her eyes were squeezed tightly closed, her white-knuckled fingers wrapped around the railing.

Holt's heart thundered in his chest. His breath came hard. "If this is another marketing scheme to get extra attention, tell me now and I'll get the hell out of here."

She opened one eye. Fractionally. Her mouth moved but not much sound came out. "Help."

With a smile teasing at the corners of his lips, he wrapped his arm securely around her waist and lifted. She didn't budge.

"You have to let go," he said softly, reassuringly.

She shook her head.

"I've got you. I won't let you fall."

A tiny whimper escaped her lips.

"You're fine now. Loosen your fingers. That's a girl. Here we go."

This time she obeyed him. Vaguely aware of cheering from the street below, he carried her into the room and set her on her feet. Her whole body trembled like the leaves of an aspen.

This was the second time today he had held her. It was becoming a habit, an addiction that would be darn hard to break. And one he imagined would escalate with the least amount of encouragement.

He kissed her forehead and cheeks, and brushed his lips to her sweet mouth. "You're safe now. It's okay," he repeated. Safe from the perils of the balcony, but not necessarily safe from him.

Her eyes glistened. "Captain H-Hook...a-attacked me."

Something mean and ugly twisted in Holt's gut. "That man you brought up to the room?" He'd kill him with his bare hands. He'd rip out his—

"No, the gull. The one with the bad foot that I felt so sorry for."

He blinked, trying to shift gears. "You were frightened by a bird?"

"A *mean* bird," she qualified stoutly, offended by his incredulous tone.

"Man, I'd hate to think what would happen if you had to face down one of my bulls."

She sniffed. "Unless they can fly, or they come marching up the side of a building twenty stories high, I doubt I'll be faced with that problem."

He tried to keep a straight face but the smile that had been threatening turned into a full-fledged grin. She was so damn stubborn and proud and brave and innocent all at the same time, a dynamite package. Born of two parts relief for her safety and one part amazement at how wildly she affected him, Holt laughed aloud.

"Don't you make fun of me," she complained.

Her scowl of disapproval made him laugh all the harder. He either had to laugh or kiss her frown away. One or the other. And kissing would lead to nothing but trouble for both of them.

He eyed the tempting shape of her lips, naturally rosy and as inviting as a prairie blossom touched with morning dew. It wouldn't take much to—

With a determined shake of his head, Holt decided what he needed was another woman. A woman who was so different from Hannah that all thoughts of her would be driven right out of his mind—including the painful, erotic ones that were making the fit of his jeans about six sizes too tight.

8

"KIDDO, YOU ARE something else again!" Filled with effervescent enthusiasm, Sam Spivak hopped around his display booth like so much bubbling champagne. "I can *guaran-damn-tee* you a job in the promotion department at Fanfare Follies. I've never seen anything like what you've pulled off at this trade show. You're a whiz, is what you are. If you're interested, just say the word."

Hannah wasn't interested. She was mortified. "It wasn't a stunt, Sam. I really got stuck out on the balcony, and I was so scared I couldn't move." Then everybody's favorite hero showed up to rescue her—and proceeded to laugh at her predicament. Or maybe he was laughing at her stupidity.

Whatever the case, it had hurt.

In school, she'd hated it when the kids had laughed at her because she couldn't throw the basketball in the hoop, or connect a bat to a baseball, no matter how hard she tried. She'd been brought to tears more than once by their teasing, though she tried never to let them know.

Ooooo. She gritted her teeth. She was going to

get even with Holt Janson for bringing her so much grief. One way or another.

The very nerve of him to walk out on her when she was still shaking like crazy from being stuck nine hundred miles up in the air! Never mind that in her heart of hearts, she'd wanted him to go on holding her forever and maybe even kiss her long and hot and deep, which would have been even dumber than playing tag with a couple of enraged, horny gulls twenty floors up.

"Even if you didn't intend it, kiddo, all that attention brought every lingerie buyer at the show right smack to your doorstep. I got so busy trying to answer their questions about your lingerie line, I was like a chicken trying to peck a corncob clean."

"I really appreciate you helping me out. I'm sorry it turned out to be such a bother."

"Don't give it another thought. You'd do the same for me, wouldn't you?"

"Yes, I would."

He settled down a little and ran both of his palms along the sides of his head to smooth his thinning hair. "So how did it go with Zimmermann?"

She smiled. "Good...I think." Assuming all of the interruptions hadn't put him off. "He said he liked my designs and would be in touch."

"Take it from an old-time salesman, you gotta close the deal and get him to sign on the dotted line before the show's over. Once you're out of sight, memories fade. Then it's like pulling teeth to get the momentum going again.''

"I'll try. *If* I get the chance." She straightened a display of bustier samples in a rainbow of colors. "How's the show going for you?"

"Hey, ol' Slick Sam knows his stuff. Landed two new accounts—big ones—and got a slew of orders for the new lines. The wife and kids will be able to eat for another six months.''

"I'm glad." She suspected the Spivak family had a gold mine in Sam, who was a born salesman.

He leaned forward confidentially. "Fact is, it helped a lot to have the booth next to the prettiest girl at the show. Thanks, kiddo. I hope we get to do this again next year. In fact, if you wouldn't think it too presumptuous of me, I'd love to be your escort for the banquet tonight. Big doings—assuming there's no one else.''

"You're sweet, and I'd be honored. I can't think of anyone else I'd rather be with tonight at the banquet." Her heart filled with affection, she leaned across the bar that separated their two booths and kissed him on the cheek. There was another man—one who would go unnamed—who she'd like to spend more time with, but he'd hardly be interested in a lingerie-trade-show banquet. Or her, for that matter. "Your wife's a lucky woman."

"Yeah." Sam's ruddy complexion colored. "That's what she keeps telling me. The kids, they've got a whole different story, and it ain't pretty."

She laughed, turned away and found herself gazing into smiling gray eyes.

"Mr. Zimm—Jonas," she corrected, fighting a blush of her own. "I didn't see you there."

He glanced from her to Sam and back again. "If I were to pick any friend in the business, Sam Spivak would be very near the top of my list. A more loyal man I'm sure you couldn't find. But I wouldn't, my dear, allow him within a hundred yards of my wife. Not with his silver tongue."

In spite of herself, laughter bubbled once more. "I'll certainly keep your advice in mind."

"Well, you should." His expression sobered and became very businesslike. "Meanwhile, I have talked with my father. I am now prepared to offer you a contract—"

Hannah's heart nearly exploded.

"—on an exclusive basis for the designs in your bridal lingerie line. Both my father and I believe Zimmer's and Hannah's Frills will make a extraordinarily profitable combination."

Hannah quite agreed. Her voice, however, seemed to have taken a sabbatical. For the life of her, she couldn't get a word out. She was simply too happy.

Pulling a sheaf of papers from the inside pocket of his immaculately tailored gray suit, Jonas said, "I took the liberty of having a contract drawn up.

I think you'll find the details quite satisfactory for our exclusive representation.''

In spite of her excitement, Hannah heard an insistent, low-key voice in her ear. ''Don't sign anything without your own attorney reviewing it.'' It was Sam's voice, uncharacteristically firm.

Her head snapped around. Under her breath, she hissed, ''You told me to get his signature on the dotted—''

''I didn't tell you to be stupid, kiddo. Zimmer's can be as cutthroat as anybody in the business.'' He nodded toward Jonas. ''Isn't that right?''

''My father still rues the day he didn't hire you, Sam. And that was twenty years ago.''

''He tried to get me for a song. I was worth more and knew it. I don't want that to happen to Hannah.''

Jonas, looking composed, passed the proposed contract to Hannah. ''Look it over and I believe you'll find it's fair, whatever Sam says. But if you or your attorneys feel that there should be changes, we're open to negotiation.''

She clasped the papers like a lifeline. *Her independence. Her future.* ''I'll do that, Jonas. Thank you. And I'll be in touch. Soon.''

As soon as Jonas was out sight, Sam raised his hand and Hannah gave him a high five. Her smile was so wide her cheeks hurt.

''You've got him on the run now, kiddo. He's

salivating, he's so anxious to get your designs. Exclusive, yet!''

"That's good, isn't it?"

"It means you're in the driver's seat. Whatever he's offered you in that contract, he'll go more. Maybe a *lot* more."

She flipped quickly through the contract, scanning incomprehensible clauses and looking at dollar amounts that were staggering. Well, maybe not that huge, she mentally corrected, trying valiantly to remain cool and businesslike. But her excitement was difficult to contain. A *real* contract, someone willing to pay her for what she had created out of her own imagination. Her own line of lingerie with her own name on it. Amazing!

"Well, Hannah, my dear..." Giving the impression that she was simply making a casual circuit of the display area, Bubbles Von Hemmelrich promenaded past Hannah's booth, then paused, her nose lifted imperiously. "It appears Zimmer's has hooked another innocent tadpole, who they will no doubt devour in due course."

"I doubt that," Hannah told her. "I may look like a tasty morsel, but I assure you, I can be quite tough when I choose to be."

A phantom smile stole across her face. "I trust Jonas's terms are generous. A young woman of your obvious talent should not sell herself short."

"I don't intend to."

"I suppose he used that old, flattering ploy of asking for exclusive rights?"

Hannah's response was a silent frown.

"I see that I have surmised correctly. In which case, if you sign that contract, you will be trapped, unable to sell your designs elsewhere even when Zimmer's elects to no longer carry your line, thus giving his favored designers an open field." Her smile was broader now and far more cruel. "Congratulations, my dear."

The gargantuan woman whirled with amazing grace and paraded off down the aisle, leaving Hannah in stunned silence. Nausea roiled in her stomach. Maybe she wasn't cut out to be a businesswoman after all. Her right brain might be capable of creating wonderful designs but, at the moment, her left brain was slogging along like an overloaded train on a railroad track going up hill.

Desperately seeking advice, she turned to Sam.

He shrugged. "She made a couple of good points."

"What do I do?"

Glancing around the showroom, he said, "I've got a buddy, Vincente DiBiasi. He had a little problem about rigging juries while he was an attorney for the mob some years back, but he's out of the slammer now and working for Cadillac Contours. In spite of everything, he's a good man. If I ask, he'll take a look at your contract. If you want."

What choice did Hannah have? She'd kill to have

a contract with Zimmer's Fine Ladies' Wear but not one that would snatch her future from her. In this case, she suspected Bubbles might actually have been giving her a warning—a warning she intended to heed.

THE TWO HOURS she spent with Vinny turned out to be an education worth every dime she might have paid to a top attorney, but when she tried to pay him, he kissed her hand and said, "*Bellisima,* for a friend of Sammy's there is no charge. I owe him more than my life. Besides—" he dipped his head modestly "—if I charge you, the bar association will throw me back into Attica for practicing without a license."

Minutes later, she went in search of Jonas with her counteroffer. To her amazement, he agreed to every item. Not only would Zimmer's carry her bridal line, they'd stock her general lingerie as well, and agreed to produce her designs for both spring and fall for at least five years, renewing the contractual amount after two years.

She was in heaven!

And, contrary to all good wisdom, the first thing she wanted to do was share her news with Holt.

Bubbling with excitement, she cruised the hotel lobby in search of her tall cowboy roommate, then checked the coffee shop. Not until she peered into the dimly lit bar did she finally spot him in a corner booth—with a woman.

Not just an ordinary woman, either, but a tall, willowy blonde who looked as though she'd stepped out of the pages of *Vogue*.

The blades of jealousy that sliced through her were so sharp and jagged, Hannah wanted to shred the woman to pieces with a pair of oversize pinking shears.

But that wasn't fair, she realized with a hasty second thought. It wasn't the gorgeous blonde's fault that Holt had lured her into conversation with his silver-blue eyes and drop-dead smile. Few women would be able to resist him. In fact, she was probably an innocent lamb he was about to lead to slaughter with his seductive ways. The poor thing probably didn't know he'd sworn off marriage and was on the rebound from Adele.

Obviously, it was up to Hannah to protect the woman from making a serious mistake. *And* in the process she'd get a small taste of revenge for the army of maintenance people Holt had sent to interrupt her business meeting.

Yes, a little retaliation would be sweet.

This would be the perfect time to put her dormant acting talents to work, the dramatic flair that Miss Aldridge had so raved about at Crookston High. A quick alteration of costume, a small change in makeup, and a prop or two, then Holt Janson wouldn't be so eager to interfere in her life again.

Or to make her dream of things that were unattainable.

HOLT SIGNALED the waitress for another beer for himself and a gin and tonic for Xena, the Warrior Princess. Actually, he thought her name was Marijane or Madelyn, but he couldn't remember. The moment she'd picked him up in the bar, he'd decided Xena was the name that fit, given her rather broad shoulders and buxom physique.

Mildly, he conceded she was a nice enough woman and attractive enough in an Amazonian way. She simply wasn't Hannah.

That he cared bugged the hell out of him.

From the corner of his eye, he caught a movement off to his left. He turned his head.

A bag lady was coming his direction, all hunched over, hair disheveled, suit jacket buttoned unevenly, her cheeks sallow and gray. He wondered why the hotel management allowed someone like that into the bar when he got the oddest feeling that he knew the woman.

Knew her rather well.

"What the hell?" he muttered.

"Did you say something, darling?" Xena asked coyly.

Riveted on the new arrival, he shook his head. It couldn't be possible....

"My dearest Holt." With a heavy sigh, Hannah plunked her overflowing shopping bags on the dark-leather seat beside him. "The children will be so glad I've found you at last."

He choked "The who?" What was she playing at dressed like that?

Hannah raised a weary face to him. "Oh, you remember, dearest. Peter, Paul, Mary, Archibald, and little Tim." She gave a loose-wristed wave of her hand. "Oh, that's right. You never saw little Timmy, did you? And he's such a sweet thing. Of course, he has a bad case of rickets because, without any child support, I haven't—"

"What the hell are you talking about?" he bellowed.

Palms planted on the table, Xena leaned toward Hannah. "Doesn't he pay child support?"

Every pair of eyes in the bar turned their direction—glaring.

"Not a single dime." Hannah exhaled a weary breath like a volcano blowing off steam. "But I wouldn't mind so much if he'd just see the children once in a while."

"Now wait a minute!" He turned to Xena, pleading, "I hardly know this woman. She's pulling your leg."

The waitress showed up with the drinks. "I've got a special place in my heart for guys who don't support their kids," she said snidely.

"Poor little Tiny Tim has never even been held by his father."

"Tiny Tim doesn't exist!"

"That's just how my ex felt about our little girl," the waitress complained.

''I can't pry a dime out my ex, either,'' Xena added. ''Would you believe—''

''Mine was even worse—''

As if he was at a tennis match, Holt's head snapped back and forth between the two women as they ragged on their former husbands. He hadn't even known Xena had a child. Not that he cared one way or the other.

He shot a glance at Hannah. Like a devilish imp, her forget-me-not eyes sparkled at the mischief she'd created.

Before he could stop her, she slid out of the booth. ''I'll tell Timmy you send your love,'' she cooed. ''Of course, it's Peter who misses you most. But he steals a few oranges from the homeless shelter now and then to help me out. Don't worry about a thing, dearest. I know we'll be just fine.''

Holt started to go after Hannah—to wring her neck. But the waitress sat down next to him and he was trapped between the Warrior Princess and Vengeful Valery, the waitress who was talking about using a machete on a crucial part of her former husband's anatomy.

On the good-news side, both women were so engrossed in their shared anger at men in general and their exes in particular, they'd entirely lost interest in him.

Counting his blessings that he hadn't gotten more thoroughly entangled with Xena—or the waitress and her machete, for that matter—Holt scrunched himself down under the table, crawled on his knees until he was out of their sight, and escaped into the lobby of the hotel in search of Hannah, only to discover he was being paged by a bellhop.

FEELING BUOYANT, and carrying a chilled champagne bottle tucked under his arm, Holt got back to the hotel room shortly before seven o'clock. He wasn't mad at Hannah any more. Hell, since Algie had finally come through with the loan, he figured a celebration was in order. And celebrating with Hannah was exactly what he had in mind.

He knew he was taking a certain amount of risk. Too much bubbly and a woman could lose her reserve. So could a man, for that matter.

But not Holt. He was confident he could stay in control of the situation. Making love to Hannah would mean nothing but trouble for both of them. She deserved better than one night of hot sex followed by a quick adiós. And instinctively he knew they would be hot together. Like a raging prairie fire.

He wasn't going to make the mistake of lighting the match and then not being able to douse the flames before they got out of control. Yes, sir, a guy like him, who'd had a bushel full of trouble with one woman, had learned to be smarter than that.

Though the room was empty, the lights were on. From behind the closed bathroom door he heard a sweet soprano voice humming an Elton John tune. Inhaling Hannah's lingering wildflower scent, Holt smiled to himself in the same way he sometimes did when a meadowlark burst into song on a bright summer morning on the prairie.

His body stirred in anticipation of the moment she'd step into the bedroom. In his mind's eye, he saw her again as he had the first time, wrapped in a white-towel sarong, her creamy shoulders as soft as satin, her cheeks rosy with embarrassment, her eyes wide in surprise. The towel had hiked up past her knees, revealing thighs made for a man to caress. She had small, delicate feet...

He cleared his throat and placed the champagne on the desk. If he kept thinking like that, he'd lose all semblance of control. By tomorrow night he'd be back on his ranch in Montana. This was no time to do something stupid.

The bathroom door opened and a vision appeared.

Not the half-naked woman he'd been envisioning, or the deviously clever bag lady he'd met that afternoon. Or even the serious, hardworking lingerie designer he'd been rooming with the past three days.

This Hannah was the picture of sophistication. Her hair was piled on top of her head in a honey-blond tangle of curls; tasteful diamond teardrop earrings sparkled and drew attention to the tempting curve of her jaw; her black lace dress, supported only by slender spaghetti straps, clung to every one of her luscious curves.

"Hi," she said tentatively. "I didn't hear you come in."

Holt snapped his sagging jaw closed. "Hi, yourself." His voice cracked. "Looks like you're, ah, going out."

"Hmm." She picked up a sequined black purse from the bed and stuffed a lipstick into it. "It's the trade-show banquet, the grand finale of the whole week."

He couldn't keep his eyes off her. And had a devil of a time keeping his hands away, too. "You, ah, going alone?" he stammered, wondering where his usual smooth-talking cowboy style had gone.

Turning to check her hair in the wall mirror, she presented him with a view of her figure in profile— the soft arch of her back, the feminine swell of her hips. "No, Sam invited me," she said with a touch of pleasure.

Holt hated Sam—whoever the hell he was!

"He's probably waiting for me downstairs now. I'm a little behind schedule."

"He'll wait." Holt all but growled the words. A man would have to be a blithering idiot not to wait for a vision like Hannah. And not to want to remove that slinky, sexy dress in the first two seconds after he saw her.

Something in his tone made Hannah turn and look sharply at him. She'd half expected him to be angry after what she'd done that afternoon. But what she saw in his eyes wasn't anger. It was far hotter than that. Dark and dangerous. So volatile it took her breath away.

Her voice thready, she said, "I guess I'd better be going. I hate to keep Sam waiting."

Like steel drawn to a magnet, she took a step toward Holt.

"I wouldn't want you to be impolite." Echoing her movement, he drew a step closer.

"He's a very nice man." She swallowed and licked her lips, tasting the fresh lipstick she'd just applied, wishing it were Holt's flavor that she could savor.

His gaze was focused intently on her mouth. "I got the loan I was looking for."

"That's…wonderful." Her impulse was to throw her arms around his neck in congratulatory hug. But that simple gesture would make her life infinitely complicated. "I got the contract I was after."

"Great. Looks like we're both going home winners."

Home. Holt to Montana, she to Minnesota. Not all that good at geography, she wondered how many thousands of miles would be separating them by tomorrow evening.

"So, ah…" His gaze slipped lower, slowly perusing her breasts and the tight fit of her dress. "I hope you've forgotten that foolishness about losing your virginity."

For an instant, she forgot to breathe. "Foolishness? It has to go sometime, doesn't it?" With the right man—with Holt—she'd rid herself of that impediment in a heartbeat.

His Adam's apple moved but he didn't utter a word, his answer to her question obvious. He still wasn't interested in doing the deed.

Abruptly, fighting an unwelcome urge to cry, she ducked past him toward the door. "Sam will be waiting. I've got to..." The rest of the words simply couldn't make it past the knot of despair that filled her throat as she escaped out the door.

Stupid woman! She'd set herself up for rejection again.

THE DAMN TUX didn't fit worth beans.

Holt tugged at the too-short sleeves. It had cost him the price of a couple of good head of beef cattle to talk one of the banquet waiters out of this getup and into changing places with him. The collar was choking him. The pants were so short they looked like they were meant for wading through spring floods, and if he bent over too far they sure as hell were going to split right down the middle.

But no way was he going to leave Hannah unchaperoned with some guy named Sam.

It was the damn virginity thing that kept eating at him. She'd be going home tomorrow and she'd as much as admitted she wanted to leave her virtue behind. And the way she was dressed...that hot look in her eyes just before she'd run from the room...

Well, he was scared spitless she was gonna do something she'd regret, get in over her head. And it would be his fault because he'd wanted to be so noble.

If anyone was going to take care of her "problem," it was damn well going to be him!

Holt hefted a tray filled with salad plates. Wincing, he felt the suit fabric strain and heard the seam under his arm pop a few threads.

"Damn cheap suit!" he muttered, stalking out through the swinging doors into the banquet room.

9

AN ASSORTMENT of lingerie salesmen vied loudly and forcefully, shoving each other like a bunch of rowdy sixth-grade boys, trying for a place at the table with Hannah and Sam. Secretly, Hannah was pleased. These past few days as Holt's roommate had been hard on her ego. Except that a few minutes ago up in their room, he had looked at her as if he wanted her. *Really* wanted her.

But she'd read him all wrong. What an innocent, naive fool he must think her.

Perhaps it was for the best.

They'd be going their separate ways after tonight. Though she'd been the one to suggest that a single night of passion—of ridding herself of her not-so-priceless virginity—would be a satisfactory arrangement, she was no longer quite so confident.

Perhaps if he hadn't so nobly refused her offer she might not have cared so much.

She might not have fallen so completely in love with the man.

Smiling wanly across the table at the salesman from Quirky Garters—or maybe he was from Sleep-Tight Nighties, she couldn't quite remember—she realized she didn't have much choice, one way or the other. No matter what happened, by tomorrow night she and Holt would be thousands of miles apart.

A waiter lifted the bright pink, fan-folded napkin from the water goblet in front of her, snapped it in the air dramatically, and slid it across her lap. In the process, his forearm brushed against the underside of her breast. *Intentionally!*

Affronted, her gaze snapped up and her mouth opened ready with an angry rebuke, which snagged in her throat.

Holt smiled down at her. "Good evening, madam. I trust you will find the service satisfactory this evening."

Regaining her voice, she hissed, "What are you doing here?"

"I thought the tips might be good." He turned to place a napkin in Sam's lap, though with far less flair.

"The *tips?*" she squeaked.

"I'm burdened with a heavy repayment schedule on this new loan I've gotten. Every little bit helps."

"Are you crazy?"

"Very possibly."

Her jaw sagging nearly to her chest, she watched Holt maneuver around the table of banquet guests, murmuring with uncharacteristic deference as he placed a napkin in each lap. The tuxedo he was wearing should have made him look like an overstuffed scarecrow, the sleeves so short his elbows were practically showing, but somehow he still managed to look like he'd just stepped out of *GQ*. His expression was oddly serene, unlike the man she'd grown to know and love in such a short period of time. More like a man who had reached some momentous decision.

But none of that changed the fact that he still walked like a long-legged cowboy.

What on earth was he up to?

The man on her left, Ralph Knutte—whom she'd mentally nicknamed Eyebrows because they were so thick and bushy—slipped his arm around the back of her chair.

"Honey, you sure do bring some much-needed class to our little party here. I was wondering... Minneapolis is part of my territory. Maybe I could give you a call next time I'm up that direction."

"I don't actually live very close to Minneapolis," she hedged.

"Traveling a few extra miles won't bother me a—"

Holt's tuxedo-clad arm shoved its way between Hannah and her neighbor. Rather than risk getting his shoulder broken by the forceful presence of the waiter, Ralph withdrew his hand from behind Hannah's chair.

"Enjoy your salad, sir," Holt said smoothly,

dropping the plate on the table with a plunk from about three inches up.

Hannah whipped her head around to look at Holt as he was about to place another salad in front of her. Unfortunately, in her surprise she'd moved too abruptly. Her head connected with the plate, tipping it slightly. Holt tried to right it, but didn't quite succeed.

Hannah's eyes widened.

In what seemed like slow motion, a black olive circled the rim of plate, teetered on the edge and dropped with the precision of a high-tech smart bomb—right into her cleavage. Icy-cold, it lodged between her breasts just out of sight.

She gasped.

Holt swore, his silver-blue gaze zeroing in on the spot where the olive had disappeared.

"Why looky there, sweet little Hannah," Ralph chortled. "You want me to retrieve that pesky ol' olive—"

"You try that, mister," Holt warned tautly, "and you'll find your arm's about a foot shorter than it used to be."

"No! Don't do that!" Heat flamed her cheeks. "I'll get it myself. Later." Much later, when there weren't so many prying eyes around her.

From her right, Sam asked, "Is everything okay, kiddo?"

She mustered a weak smile. "Fine. Thank you."

Warily, her gaze tracked Holt to the far side of the table as he served the salads.

When she felt he was at a safe distance, she risked a bite of lettuce.

"Allow me, madam," he said, appearing like magic at her elbow. "Some dressing?"

She froze. "Why don't I serve myself this time?"

"I assure you, madam, hotel management wants to make your meal—"

"You drip any of that oily stuff on my brand-new dress and you'll pay the cleaning bill," she threatened.

"Consider yourself in safe hands, my dear." Deftly, he spooned dressing over her salad.

"Where did you learn to be a waiter?" she whispered suspiciously.

"My misspent youth. I worked my way through college waiting tables at a greasy spoon. Taught me a lot about people, which is why I decided I'd stick to working with cattle."

"Oh." She hadn't considered Holt might have done anything other than ranching, and she found it admirable that he'd put himself through school. But it seemed like an odd time for him to revisit his former occupation.

"Hey, fella, you gonna let the rest of us have any of the salad dressing?" Ralph asked.

Holt visibly tensed as though eyeing a new target, shifting the boat of oily salad dressing at a precarious angle in the general direction of Ralph's lap.

"Don't you dare!" Hannah muttered under her breath.

Snarling something inaudible, Holt placed the silver dish on the table and stalked away.

Relieved, Hannah exhaled.

"Nothin' I hate more than an uppity waiter," Ralph complained, his bushy eyebrows caterpillaring into a straight line. "I oughta report him to his boss, that's what I oughta do. Get him fired in a hurry."

"Don't bother. I don't think our waiter intends this job to be a lifetime career."

A few moments later, generous man that he was, Sam Spivak ordered a couple of bottles of wine for the table. His tux was a bit out of the ordinary—a garish red, green and yellow plaid that on Sam looked good. Almost distinguished.

Holt dutifully filled the glasses—all except Hannah's. In hers he poured no more than a thimbleful.

"That's it?" she asked quietly when he lingered next to her chair.

"I don't want you getting drunk."

"I'm a big girl, Holt. I'm sure I can handle a whole glass this one time without any ill effects."

"I don't want to take any chance that you'll get tipsy, not with these lounge lizards—" he pointedly looked in Ralph's direction "—hanging all over you."

If she hadn't known better, Hannah would have thought Holt's bizarre behavior stemmed from jealousy. But that didn't seem possible. He had, after all, rejected her earlier overtures. It seemed, in his eyes, being virginal was a decided disadvantage for a woman.

Although his philosophy might have changed, she thought, recalling how he'd behaved earlier in their room. There was a gleam in his eyes she wasn't sure how to decipher.

As the men at the table finished their salads, Holt snatched up the plates, barely giving them a chance to put down their forks. He wanted this banquet over and he wanted it over in a hurry.

He'd never made a fool of himself over any woman, not even his former wife. And she'd done her damnest to wrap him around her little finger.

But that's what he was doing now. Being a fool. Like a greenhorn trying to ride a rodeo bronc. And he couldn't stop himself.

With a determined set of his jaw, he vowed he was going to be the man who retrieved that olive from between Hannah's soft breasts. He'd do it with his lips, his tongue, and he'd damn well taste every salty little bite he intended to take.

No other guy was gonna come close. Not while he was still standing.

Hefting the tray filled with dirty dishes, he gritted his teeth. This damn banquet was gonna be the longest two hours of his entire life.

To HANNAH'S amazement, Holt served the main course of chicken in a cream sauce, baby potatoes and asparagus spears without incident. No plates slid into anyone's lap. Water glasses were filled promptly, if without a lot of grace. But every time she glanced around, he was there. Hovering.

She tried to follow the conversation at the table—of sales made, shifting territories and bankruptcies in the offing. It wasn't easy to concentrate with Holt's silver-blue eyes boring a twin pair of holes in the back of her skull.

"Is there something wrong with our waiter?" Sam finally asked under his breath.

"He's not a waiter," she whispered in response. "He's my roommate, the man I told you about."

"Ah." He nodded knowingly. "That explains everything."

It didn't explain anything to Hannah, but she let the thought go as the trade-association president got up to begin the evening's program. Ralph scooted his chair around closer to Hannah's in order to get a better view of the podium. Almost casually, he hooked his arm around the back of her chair again.

He leaned his head close to hers. In her ear he whispered, "This is great, huh?"

Hannah held her breath. She didn't dare look to see where Holt was or what he was doing. Instead, she hoped whatever affliction had overtaken him wouldn't result in some totally humiliating scene.

After briefly introducing special guests, the president said, "While we're waiting for our desserts to be served, we have a special honor to present, one we don't always award. This year I'm sure you'll all agree we have an exceptional candidate for this unique tribute." He held up an engraved plaque that glistened in the spotlight. "For our much coveted Rookie of the Year award—"

As he paused dramatically, all eyes swung toward Hannah's table.

Puzzled, she glanced around at those who were seated with her.

"The unanimous choice is Hannah Jansen of Hannah's Frills, the beautiful young lady who has captured all of our hearts with her winning smile...and incidentally with her creative lingerie designs as well."

The audience burst into wild applause; the men at her table stood and cheered.

Dumbstruck, Hannah thought for sure she was going to cry. Barely able to rise to her feet, she shook her head and said to Sam, "This was your doing, wasn't it?"

With a embarrassed shrug, as though he'd been caught with his fingers in the cookie jar, he brushed a kiss to her cheek. "You deserve it, kiddo. You're the best."

She kissed him back, somehow made it to the podium and managed with an emotion-choked voice to express her thanks. She'd never realized how dear a group of semirowdy lingerie salesmen and designers could become to her in such a short time. They'd all been so very, very kind to her.

When she left the stage, Holt was there at the steps to offer his hand to steady her.

"Congratulations," he whispered. "I'm proud of you."

Her eyes misted with tears again. If she'd been given a choice, she would have willingly traded this wonderful honor for one night in Holt's arms. But that wasn't to be.

To continuing applause, he escorted her back to the table and then released her, stepping away while her friends added their best wishes.

Ralph, not satisfied with mere words, grabbed her in a bear hug and kissed her soundly on the mouth. He tasted vaguely of asparagus.

"That's it!" Holt bellowed. "You're coming with me." With a yank, he took her hand and started to drag her away.

"I haven't had dessert," she complained. "It's chocolate cheese—"

"Forget it," he countered forcefully.

"Now wait a minute," Ralph protested. "What the hell do you think you're doing?"

Instead of responding to Ralph, Holt nailed Hannah with a look that brooked no argument. "I'm going to take care of that little problem of yours, Hannah Jansen—with an *e*. And I'm going to do it *now*."

Holt tugged on her to go one direction; Ralph pulled her the opposite way.

She clutched the plaque to her chest. "My problem?" she echoed.

"Yeah. You know. Your *problem*. The one you want to get rid of."

Her eyes widened. Excitement and anticipation collided somewhere in her midsection. "*That* problem?"

"Yeah. *That* problem. Let's get out of here."

"Wait just one darn minute." Ralph tried to arm wrestle her away from Holt but he was outweighed, out-toughed, and less determined than the tuxedo-wearing cowboy. He did manage to snag a handful of the sleeve of Holt's jacket, however. With a loud rip, it came off in his hand. He stared at it stupidly.

Meanwhile, Holt reached behind him and picked up a pitcher of ice-cold water from a serving tray. With a flourish, he dumped it over Ralph's head. "Mister, I've been wanting to do that all evening. Now keep your paws off of me and my girl. You got that?"

His girl? The thrill of triumph shimmered through Hannah.

Ralph spluttered a vile string of curses.

Several men stood and moved threateningly toward Holt.

Sam said to Hannah, "If I had to guess, I'd say this was a good time for me to get some of the boys to ply the Corset Queen with a few Rocky Mountain Mudslides.''

As Holt made a strategic retreat with Hannah in tow, she sent Sam a quick grin. "Yes, please, about a dozen if you can manage it." She wouldn't want to disturb her next-door neighbor, and she thought it might be a long night. A gloriously long night, if she had her way.

10

HIS HAND SHOOK as he slid the card key into the lock.

Holt had expected Hannah to be nervous. But not him. He'd made love hundreds of times with maybe a dozen or more women.

This time was different. Important in ways that he couldn't even name.

Opening the door, he followed Hannah inside. He felt slightly light-headed, as if he'd run up twenty flights of stairs instead of riding an elevator with a knot gnawing away in his stomach and the cat keeping a firm hold on his tongue.

In the center of the room, she turned and looked up at him. The trust in her eyes, the totally innocent belief that she'd be safe with him, nearly brought him to his knees.

He took the Rookie of the Year plaque that she'd been clinging to like a shield, placed it on the desk, then cradled her face between his palms as tenderly as if she were a fragile prairie wildflower. In contrast to her delicate features, his hands looked big and awkward. God, how could he be gentle enough not to hurt her?

"Hannah, are you sure—absolutely sure this is what you want?"

"Absolutely."

"If you want to say no, I'll understand." Though it would probably kill him if he couldn't kiss her, taste her sweet flavor, bury himself in the soft folds of her secret center.

A frown creased her forehead. "Have you changed your mind?"

"Hell, no," he said gruffly. "I want you so much it hurts."

"I'm glad." A sweet smile replaced her frown and her hands slid up his lapels. She brushed a single finger across his lips, sending a tremor of pure unadulterated need through him. "I'm not exactly sure what to do, though, so you'll have to show me."

"Yeah." He swallowed thickly. "I can do that."

First he wanted to release the pins from her hair so it would hang loose, like silk. Then he would kiss her. Oh, yeah, kiss her till she trembled in his arms as wildly as he was already shaking. If he was going to spin out of control, he wanted Hannah that way, too.

He wanted to pleasure her as no woman had ever been pleasured; he wanted to teach her all of the textures and flavors a woman could enjoy with a man. He wanted to take his time with her, though he wasn't sure he could.

But he was damn well going to try.

Hannah exhaled as he removed the pins from her hair. She'd had no idea the nerve endings along the back of her neck could be so sensitive to a man's touch—to Holt's touch, she mentally qualified. His warm breath skimming over her heated cheeks had a sweet scent to it. Sugared coffee, she thought dimly. His gaze was so intense, she found herself fascinated by the darkening blue of his eyes, the curl of his lashes, the tiny squint lines at the corners.

And then she couldn't see anything at all as he lowered his head and his mouth covered hers. She could only feel. His heat. His strength. The demands of his tongue as it slid deftly between her lips.

Exquisite sensations rippled through her, of wanting and longing and feeling that she was standing on the brink of some new discovery that had eluded her for years. Her knees grew weak.

When his mouth left hers, she felt momentarily bereft. But her groan of objection turned to another sigh as his teeth nibbled lightly along the column of her neck. He slid the straps from her shoulders and kissed her there, too, gently biting and sucking and making her tremble. Her zipper hummed downward, echoed by shivers that sped along her spine.

"Holt?" Her voice faltered and she clung to his shoulders.

"Shh, sweetheart, I've been envying that darn olive all night. When I find it, it's a goner."

She gasped as his search took his lips on an intimate trail that led between her breasts. "Oh, my…"

"I'll share," he murmured, plucking the olive from its hiding place in the curve of her strapless bra.

He fused their mouths together again and she tasted him and the olive and a flavor she thought might be her own. Spicy and tangy, sweet and sharp, the combined essence swirled through her senses, intoxicating her in a way that no wine could ever be.

Vaguely she became aware that her dress had pooled at her feet, snaring her, and she wasn't quite sure how that had happened.

"Great garters," Holt murmured, his callused palm caressing her upper thigh. With exquisite care, he unhooked one silk stocking and began to roll it down her leg. The brush of his fingers burned a fiery path along her extraordinarily sensitive flesh.

"Exclusive from Hannah's Frills," she whispered, barely able to endure the building pleasure and anticipation, growing more eager by the minute, and more frustrated. "Holt, could you…I want to touch you, too. I want to see you. All of you." Desperate to steady herself on legs that had gone as weak as water, Hannah threaded her fingers through his hair.

"Sure."

She wanted to help him undress, but her fingers

felt clumsy and uncoordinated, exploring haphaz-
ardly his magnificent male body as he shed one
piece of clothing after another. The hair on his chest
twined around her fingers; his hips were cowboy-
lean, his arms muscular. His arousal—

"Oh, my Lord..." she groaned.

He chuckled softly. "I promise you, sweetheart,
we'll fit together like a glove."

Her gaze snapped up to meet his reassuring
smile. "I guess I'll have to take your word for it."

"No, I'm going to show you. There, in that
bed."

As she glanced over her shoulder, she was struck
by a sudden case of shyness. But Holt didn't waver.
She simply followed his lead, details blurring in the
midst of a new world of sensation.

He laid her on the bed, the sheets cool on her
back, his caresses hot on her flesh. He kissed her
and stroked her in ways she hadn't known possible,
taking her on a journey of sensual delight. She
wanted him to hurry; she wanted the experience to
go on forever.

"Please, Holt..." She arched up to him.

He covered her with another rain of fiery kisses.
"There's no reason to rush, sweetheart. I want this
to be special. *You're* special."

She clung to him and kissed him, wanting to give
back some of the pleasure he was giving her, a
pleasure so sharp and exquisite it almost hurt.

"You make me feel so—" The breath left her—

all reason left her—when he kissed her more intimately than she had ever imagined a man could. Her body bucked and she cried out his name.

When he finally entered her, the slight stab of pain she experienced was nothing compared to the feeling of joy that she had at last come home.

LATER, her body still throbbing in the afterglow of one shattering climax after another—all of the rockets and fireworks a woman dreamed about—she cuddled next to him and he held her tight. With the drapes open onto the balcony, Hannah could see the single eye of the moon gazing in. Winking, she thought.

"Hmm," she sighed, "I'm glad you didn't let me get drunk."

He toyed with the damp strands of hair at her temple. "How's that?"

"I wouldn't have wanted to forget any of this. Not one single thing."

"Me, too."

Her head resting on her chest, she smiled. "So when do I get to taste-test the chocolate?"

"Chocolate?"

"It's always been my favorite flavor. Well, rocky-road ice cream, anyway. I'd do almost anything for that. And you did make me miss the cheesecake."

"After what we just did, I'm a little brain-dead, sweetheart. What are you talking about?"

She giggled. "The rest of the condoms you have stashed in the drawer, silly. The *chocolate* ones. I assume you bought them for a reason."

He went very still and she wondered if she'd said something wrong.

"You want to do that?" he asked in a hoarse voice.

Lifting her head, she gazed into his eyes. "I want to do everything with you, Holt. Everything the law allows and then some. Remember, we only have this one night." And she vowed she wouldn't beg for more, no matter how much she wanted to.

THE COOING of Captain Hook and his girlfriend on the balcony woke them at midmorning.

They hadn't gotten much sleep, their lovemaking growing more intense with each passing hour as dawn approached—along with the time their respective planes would depart for far different destinations.

Holt had never known a more passionate woman. She was so responsive, so eager, he'd been hard-pressed to keep up. Yet even now, just watching her as she pulled on her slacks, concealing her high-cut panties from his view, he wanted her again.

And she was getting ready to leave.

Tugging on his shirt, he had a crazy urge to lock her in their room and never let her go. At least not until he'd gotten himself back under control—say in a year or two from now.

Sitting in the desk chair to put on her shoes, Hannah caught sight of the forgotten bottle of champagne. "Oops, looks like we forgot to celebrate our contracts." She was proud her voice sounded so cheerful, not all weepy like the feelings she was valiantly trying to suppress. She was *not* going to beg or plead; she'd promised him that. He'd given her the one night she'd asked for; she wouldn't ask for more.

"I got about all the celebration I could handle last night," he replied meaningfully.

A ripple of pleasure fluttered through her and she smiled, in spite of herself. "So did I." Though she'd be happy enough to celebrate in the same way every night for the rest of her life. That, however, didn't appear to be an option. "So when do you start building your herds?" she asked, refusing to dwell on things that couldn't be.

"I'll spend the rest of the summer installing a fence for the deer pen and pick up a small starter herd by this fall. Meanwhile, I'll round up whatever buffalo I can find already grazing my land and brand 'em. It'll be three or four years before I can do any harvesting. Except for the antlers, of course. Us old guys have to stock up on those."

"Trust me on this, Holt. If your performance last night was any example, you won't be needing any boost from aphrodisiacs for a lot longer than four years."

With a grin, he dipped his head in acknowledgement of the compliment, sending a lock of unkempt hair sliding across his forehead. "I appreciate your vote of confidence, madam."

Her fingers itched to comb the strands back into place. "I only relate the facts, kind sir. Even in my wildest dreams, I hadn't imagined—" Her throat clogged on a lump of unwelcome emotion and she lowered her head, feigning enormous interest in her shoes. However was she going to leave him and retain any semblance of dignity?

"So how 'bout you? What's next in the lingerie business?"

She gratefully pursued the change of subject. "Jonas is arranging for me to meet with his manufacturing people in the next couple of weeks. If all goes well, Hannah's Frills ought to debut in Zimmer's flagship store in time for Christmas."

"Hey, that's great. You must be excited."

"Thrilled. I accomplished everything I wanted on this trip. Everything..." Her voice trailed off as she met his gaze.

His brows lowered and his eyes held an expression of concern. "Including losing your virginity."

"Yes, that too," she whispered.

"Are you sorry?"

"No, never that." Not if she lived to be a thousand would she stop cherishing the memories of last night, her first and only night with Holt Janson— with an *o*.

"Look, about last night—"

Abruptly, she came to her feet. She didn't want to deal with an apology, or be reminded he wasn't the marrying kind. She knew all that. Hearing it again wouldn't help a bit.

"Will you just look at the time?" she asked with forced animation. "I've still got to get packed and get my sample case ready and here we are, dawdling. I sure hope my father remembers to pick me up at Grand Forks. It's a long walk home—"

"I'll go to the airport with you and hang around until my flight leaves."

Her head snapped up. "No! It'll be easier if we say goodbye here." A lingering farewell would have her blubbering by the time she got on the plane—not that she was likely to avoid a few tears anyway.

"At least let me see you downstairs and into a cab. You haven't even eaten yet. I could buy you breakfast. Or lunch."

"I'm not hungry." If she put anything down her throat, she'd probably choke.

He jammed his fingertips into the front pockets of his incredibly tight-fitting jeans, pulling the zipper taut across his lean hips. In wonder and awe, Hannah remembered in extraordinary detail what a big man he was when fully aroused, and how amazingly well they had fit together. Two parts of a puzzle that had been made for each other...except he wasn't likely to believe that.

She blew out a frustrated sigh. She'd known from

the beginning what she was getting herself into. Too late now to cry over a few broken threads.

"All right, if you insist, but I *will* see you to the cab downstairs," he announced. "You can't stop me from doing that."

With a courageous smile playing at the corners of her lips, she agreed. At least Holt—and any of the trade-show participants who might be in the vicinity of the hotel entrance—would catch a glimpse of the grand finale she'd planned. In some small way that would buoy her spirits. For a while.

A MOB of departing guests crowded around the hotel exit waiting for cabs to pull into the curved driveway.

Asking Holt to watch her bags, Hannah found the bell captain and slipped him a generous tip. "If you can manage it, I'd like to have a station wagon instead of a sedan for my cab."

He glanced at the money she'd given him and smiled. "Of course, miss. I'm sure I can arrange that."

Within minutes the bell captain had flagged down a cab that would meet her needs quite nicely.

"I'd like my sample case tied on top," she told the cabby.

He gave her a surly look. "There's plenty of room inside, lady. It's just you—"

"Please," she said sweetly. "With the labels showing, if you will."

Suspicious, Holt frowned. "What are you up to?"

She gave him one of her Cheshire-cat smiles, one that suggested she was about to devour a very tasty morsel. "Wait and watch. I told you from the beginning, no matter what happened I planned to go out of here with a bang. No one's likely to forget Hannah's Frills after this."

Holt wasn't likely to forget Hannah at all. He couldn't believe she was simply going to get in a cab, drive away and he'd never see her again. A normal woman would put up some sort of a fuss, especially after the dynamite sex they'd shared together. A few tears would be in order. Plans to get together again, maybe next year.

Women *always* confused good sex with love. It was in their nature, damn it!

But no, Hannah was busily getting ready to pull off another one of her marketing stunts. Evidently she'd already put their one-night stand behind her.

Holt couldn't. And it irritated the hell out of him that she so easily could.

Some cowboy! Ha!

Pulling his Stetson down lower to shade his eyes, he watched morosely as she directed the cabby on exactly how he should tie her sample case on the car roof.

Nearby there was a little flurry of activity, and the guy who'd been sitting next to Hannah at the banquet, the one who'd been wearing the out-of-sight plaid tuxedo, pushed his way through the crowd.

"Hey, kiddo," he called to Hannah. "You're weren't going to go off without saying goodbye, were you?"

"Oh, Sam, I'm sorry." She opened her arms and they embraced. The guy kissed her on the cheek.

It was all Holt could do not to pick the jerk up by the scruff of the neck and toss him into Lake Michigan.

Controlling the urge with difficulty, he asked Hannah, "This is Sam? I thought Sam was the other guy at the table, the one who spent half the night trying to maul you."

"Oh, no, that was Ralph. I didn't even know him." She laughed lightly, like spring rain dancing across a pond. "This is my friend Sam, of Fanfare Follies. He's very special to me."

Holt wanted to be special to her, too.

"You'll keep in touch, won't you, kiddo?"

"Of course I will, Sam."

The balding guy looked up at Holt, then back at Hannah. "So how'd it go last night? All quiet?"

A blush turned Hannah's cheeks scarlet, and probably did the same thing to Holt's from the heat he felt. *Quiet?* Not likely. Hannah's passionate cries had been enough to rouse the dead and had propelled Holt over the brink more than once.

"We didn't hear a peep out of next door," she

told Sam, color still flaming her cheeks. "Thanks. A lot."

"Glad to help out." He turned to Holt and extended his hand. "You're a lucky man, Mr. Janson. I hope you know that."

Not quite sure what to make of this entire conversation, which seemed to be in code, Holt shook hands. "Yeah, thanks," he muttered.

After another quick kiss on Hannah's cheek, Sam backed off. In the nick of time, Holt decided, his fingers flexing into fists.

"Guess that's it, then," she said brightly to Holt. "I'm ready to go."

"Not quite." Holt wasn't going to let her leave without making damn sure she remembered him and remembered him good.

He snared her with one arm, hauled her up against his chest and brought his mouth down hard on hers. When she gasped in surprise, he plunged his tongue inside. She tasted of everything a man dreamed about—hot nights, a willing woman. Passion beyond belief. And sweet, sexy innocence all rolled into one.

And she was leaving.

Damn! A grown man wasn't supposed to cry.

When he finally broke the kiss, he thought he saw a quick flash of regret in her eyes. Then, with a blink, it was gone.

"Goodbye, Holt. I can't imagine ever having a

better roommate." She lifted her stubborn little chin. "Thanks for everything."

In another instant, she'd ducked into the waiting cab and he couldn't see her face any longer, though he was left with the impression of eyes glistening with what could be tears. But he couldn't be sure.

As he stared after her, the cab bounced hard over the speed bump near the end of the driveway. On the car roof, a flap flew open on the Hannah's Frills sample case, something went pop! and paper streamers burst into the air like a skyrocket. They exploded in a rainbow of colors, falling back to drape the cab in a cheerful pile of paper camouflage.

The crowd hanging around the hotel entrance cheered and laughed. Hannah waved out the car window.

Damned if Holt didn't have to wipe a tear from his eye. His Hannah Jansen—with an *e*—was one smart lady. *Nobody* at this trade show would ever forget her.

When the noise quieted down, someone shouted, "Hey, look up there."

Craning his neck like everyone else, Holt looked up the side of the hotel—to about the twentieth floor. A very large woman, who could only be the Corset Queen, was standing on the balcony screaming, "I'm going to get you for this, Spivak! From now on, your name is mud!"

"What's she waving in her hand?" Holt asked the man in question.

"An ice bag, I'd guess. For her head. Rocky Mountain Mudslides go down easy, but are hell to deal with the next day."

Holt puzzled over that comment for a minute, still staring up at Bubbles on the balcony, then asked, "Tell me, Sam, what did you mean about me being a lucky man?"

"It'd take a real fool not to know the answer to that one, Mr. Janson. Hannah loves you. In my book, that makes you about the luckiest man in the world."

HANNAH WAITED until the cab had turned the corner beyond the hotel and then, in spite of the vow she'd made to herself, an uncontrollable sob burst from her throat. Tears coursed down her cheeks like a summer rainstorm. Her chest burned with a shattering pain that could only be a broken heart.

Holt had been right.

She wasn't the kind of woman who could handle a one-night stand.

She wanted marriage and children and a ranch house beneath the big Montana sky.

She wanted Holt. Forever.

He'd told her it wouldn't work.

Why hadn't she believed him?

11

DUST SWIRLED across the prairie and a blistering summer sun beat down on Holt's back. In contrast, the air-conditioning in the Towers Hotel in Chicago would have felt as frigid as a blizzard whipping across the winter landscape.

Sweat beading his forehead, Holt shifted and slammed the gasoline-powered posthole digger into gear. The spinning drill ate through the topsoil, tossing up clods of rich, fragrant dirt. He ignored the scent, wishing instead he could smell the wildflowers that reminded him of Hannah. The memory of her had been boring a hole in his stomach for the past week.

Sam Spivak had been wrong.

If Holt had been a lucky man, Hannah would be at the ranch house now, waiting for him.

But he wasn't the marrying kind. And she didn't deserve to be stranded out here on a remote ranch where talking to cows and maybe a few prairie dogs was a full-time occupation. That was the lesson his ex-wife had taught him.

Except Hannah was different.

"Yeah, different," he mumbled. She had a whole

new career in front of her, one so compelling she hadn't even looked back when she'd driven away from the hotel in that cab, streamers flying.

Lucky? Hell, it was about as *un*lucky as any man could be to have fallen in love with Hannah Jansen.

That thought—the one that contained that totally uncharacteristic word *love*—jarred him like a bronc who'd landed hard on spraddled legs. It almost drove him into the ground.

Could he have fallen in love with Hannah that quickly? Was there any other possibility?

His hand trembling on the gearshift, he swore long and hard and with great feeling.

"You plannin' to dig a hole to China?" his foreman shouted at him over the roaring noise of the drill.

Abruptly, Holt backed the motor into reverse and eased the drill out of the hole that he'd dug way too deep. Only halfway to China. "Toss some dirt in there," he ordered grumpily.

Thumbing the brim of his Stetson upward a notch, Skeeter Williams eyed Holt speculatively. His foreman was about as old as the Montana hills and had probably ridden over most of them on a rangy cow pony that he'd broken himself. Hired hand or not, he wasn't a man to take much guff from anyone.

"Thought you was gonna get that itch scratched whiles you was in Chicago," he accused.

"I did." Holt hefted a post from the stack in the

back of the pickup and rested it on his shoulder. Skeeter couldn't even begin to imagine how well he'd scratched that itch for one single night. A memorable night. One he wouldn't soon forget.

"Made things worse, huh?"

"Yeah." Much worse. Holt couldn't wake up in the morning without thinking of Hannah and wanting her there in his bed with him. Most nights he had a hell of time getting to sleep at all. And every time he caught sight of a wildflower blooming on the prairie, he thought of her. Smelled her. Tasted her.

It was driving him crazy.

Laconically, Skeeter shoveled loose dirt into the hole. "So you figure putting in this fool fence is gonna help?"

"It's for the deer herd. You know that."

"Yep. But what else I knows is that you're thinking hard on something with two legs, not four."

Holt slid the metal post from his shoulder into the hole. Skeeter had that damn straight. Hannah had the most glorious pair of legs he'd ever seen—or had ever had wrapped around his waist. He remembered when they'd been taking their shower together and he'd lifted her—

"It ain't that lawyering woman you're mooning over, is it?"

He mentally shook his head to wipe away the image of Hannah in his arms, the memory of sinking himself into her soft, sweet body. "Nope."

"Who's this one?"

"She designs lingerie."

A smile stretched the leathery skin across Skeeter's prominent cheekbones. "I like the sound of that."

So did Holt. "Doesn't matter. This ranch is no place for a woman. It's too remote, too lonely."

"Some could manage. Fact is—" He used the shovel handle to pack the loose, red dirt into the hole while Holt kept the post straight. "This ain't the only place you could raise deer, neither. It's jest the place you wanna be."

Holt stared at his foreman—his friend and companion for more years than he could count—and wondered at the jolt of possibility that zapped through him like summer lightning. The ranch was his life. Since he'd been a kid, this was where he'd wanted to live; ranching was what he wanted to do.

But Hannah was what he wanted more than anything his muddled mind could comprehend. Without her, there was no life.

Removing his hat, Holt swiped the sweat from his forehead. "Could you hold down the fort for a few more days till I can, ah, work out a few details?" he asked his foreman.

Skeeter shucked another shovel full of dirt into the hole, bringing the level pretty close to the brim. He tamped it down. "If you kin get your itch scratched real good this time, it'd be worth it. You've been as mean as a grizzly bear with a thorn up his rear end since you come back from Chicago.''

Holt resisted the urge to hug the old man. The
fact that he loved ol' Skeeter Williams like a favorite uncle wasn't something a macho guy needed
to advertise.

What he did need was to find the quickest, most
direct flight to Grand Forks, and then rent a car that
would take him to Crookston. He'd already wasted
too much time acting like an overachieving gopher,
digging holes he suddenly didn't give a damn
about.

Hannah Jansen—with an *e*—was far more important to him than any herd of deer. Or cattle, for
that matter. If he could get her into his arms again,
and into his bed, and keep her there, he'd be more
than a hundred years old before he'd be in the market for even a trace of ground-up deer antlers to
pump him up.

"I'M AFRAID I'll electrocute myself. Leroy says I
will and that I should wait till he can do it. But he
never finds the time."

"Don't worry about it, Marilou, putting in a dimmer switch is easy.'' Hannah gave the young housewife a reassuring smile, though she knew Marilou
wasn't the handiest person in town with a screwdriver and pair of pliers. But for the past week it
had been easier to think about other people's trou-

bles than to dwell on her own—namely a broken heart that didn't want to heal.

"I didn't exactly get it right when I tried to change the washer on the kitchen sink."

"A flooded kitchen isn't the worst thing that can happen. The fire department got the water turned off, didn't they?" *Eventually*, Hannah recalled, repressing a smile. "This time just be sure you get the electricity turned off before you begin."

"How do I know which one of those little fuse switchy things to turn off?"

"That's easy. Turn on the lamp that's on the circuit that you're going to change and start throwing switches at the fuse box. When the light goes out, you know you've found the right one."

"Oh, Hannah, you're so smart."

"Not exactly," she mumbled, more to herself than to Marilou. If she'd been smart she would have known one night of passionate lovemaking with Holt would never be enough; she would have known how to protect her heart; and she wouldn't have driven away from that hotel sobbing so hard the cabby wouldn't even let her pay the fare. He'd also threatened to go back to the Towers and flatten Holt's face.

As she rang up Marilou's dimmer switch on the cash register, she smiled at the memory of the cabby. The dear man had been so worried about her.

But she'd be all right. She had to be. There really wasn't any other choice.

The bell on the front door chimed and Terence Jansen strode in. He wasn't a big man, and his middle had gone soft from too much home cooking, but there was still a spring in his step. "Afternoon, Marilou. You findin' everything you need?"

"You bet, Mr. Jansen. Hannah's a whiz. My hubby's going to be so impressed when he comes home from work and finds out I changed the light switch all by myself."

"Hannie's a good one, she is." He slipped behind the old wooden counter with its clutter of displays—glow-in-the-dark night-lights in elfin shapes, a basket of marked-down Christmas ornaments left over from the season Hannah's high-school class was raising extra money for their prom, and key chains sporting every possible car model built prior to this decade. *Nothing* was ever thrown out at Jansen's Hardware.

The door chimed again, admitting Margaret Clausen.

"Hello, Hannie, dear. And Terence. How nice." With as much coyness as a teenager, she fluttered her eyelashes. "I was hoping you'd be here."

"Just got in," he grumbled with more embarrassment than anger.

"I'm so glad," Margaret cooed.

Watching in amusement as her father flushed, it occurred to Hannah that Margaret had probably been parked on the street, spying, waiting for Terence to return from his errands at the bank before she came inside.

Hannah gave Marilou her change and dropped the dimmer switch into a brown paper bag. "If you have any problems, give me a call." Surely this was one repair job Marilou could handle, however poor her track record had been until now.

"Thanks, I will." Marilou shot a curious glance at the two senior-citizen lovebirds.

Repressing a smile, Hannah shrugged. It'd be nice if someone in her family found a happily-ever-after romance. In this case, knowing her father was well cared for would release Hannah to pursue her own dreams. *All the way to Montana,* if she was so inclined. Not that she'd been invited.

"Well, thanks again," Marilou said. "Good to see you, Mrs. Clausen. You, too, Mr. Jansen."

Turning away to restock the switches that Marilou had not selected, Hannah heard the door chime again and assumed it was the young woman departing.

"Terence, dear, I was wondering if you—and Hannah, too, of course—would like to come to dinner tonight. I've baked another peach pie and made up a new batch of that spaghetti sauce that you liked so much."

"Guess we could do that," Terence replied.

As if her father hadn't been at Margaret's house for dinner almost every night since she'd been home, Hannah mused. "Thanks, Margaret," she said over her shoulder. "But I've got some work I have to do on my designs." Work she hadn't been able to get to because of her obligations to Jansen's Hardware. But soon her father would retire, and she'd make darn sure the store was sold to someone else. She had her own business now, a career—

"Hannie, girl, you want to take care of the customer?"

Sure, why not? she thought with a mild taste of resentment. Since her father's love life was going so well, he hardly had time for the store at all.

She glanced across the counter and for an instant her breath caught. Then, pleasure so sharp and sweet she nearly collapsed with the joy of it sped through her.

Her mouth moved but not a sound came out. Vaguely she was aware of a broad-shouldered, lean-legged cowboy wearing boots and a black Stetson, but mostly she was fixed on silver-blue eyes that riveted her in place.

"Mr. Jansen? I'm Holt Janson—with an *o*." Removing his hat, he extended his hand to Hannah's father. "I'd like to borrow your daughter for the next sixty or seventy years or so."

"Beg pardon?"

"Oh, isn't that sweet," Margaret said with a sigh.

Hannah stared at him dumbly. "You what?"

He placed a grocery-store sack on the counter.

"You think you and I could go some place and talk awhile? There's a gallon of rocky-road ice cream in there."

Her eyes widened as she recalled Holt's stash of condoms. And how many they had used. "Chocolate. My favorite flavor."

His grin made her pulse leap. "Yeah, I know."

"Hannie, girl, it's an hour or more till closing. You can't go off—"

"Margaret will help you with the store, Dad. This is something I really need to do."

"Oh, I'd love to, Terence. You can show me how the cash register works and how..."

Unconcerned even if the store had to be closed down for the afternoon—or forever—Hannah didn't wait a moment longer for permission to leave. Her heart hammering in her chest, she slipped from behind the counter and went out the door with Holt.

He took her hand, his fingers cold from carrying the ice cream. And strong. So very strong. "Is there someplace private we can go?"

"There's a park down by the river. It's not far."

The few pedestrians on the street eyed them speculatively. Cowboys weren't exactly the norm for Crookston. Neither was seeing Hannah walking on clouds, she suspected.

"I didn't expect to see you again," she said, almost in a whisper.

"I couldn't stay away."

The feeling of elation his words brought Hannah

lifted her a few more feet off the pavement. Another remark like that and she'd be floating so high off the ground, she'd never come down. Indeed, she wouldn't want to.

It was a hot, humid day, but beneath the towering maples in the park there was a slight cooling breeze blowing off the river. The leaves fluttered gently, in contrast to Hannah's wildly pulsating heart.

He tossed the ice-cream sack on an unoccupied picnic table, leaned against the roughly hewn wood and pulled her between his legs, into the cradle of his hips. "Oh, God, Hannah, I've missed you."

His kiss was so sweet and hot, Hannah thought she might melt. With Holt, that would be heaven.

His tongue plundered her welcoming mouth. She matched him stroke for stroke. It was as if they had been apart for years, not simply a few days. It was as if her other half, that part of her that she'd sought for so long, the part that would make her whole, had suddenly reappeared. She nearly wept at the joy of it all.

When he finally broke the kiss, his breath was as raspy and labored as hers.

"I'm a little slow, Jansen, but I finally figured it out."

Her mind not entirely in gear, she echoed, "Figured what out?"

"Minnesota is deer country, isn't it?"

She'd been thinking passionate lovemaking, a lifetime commitment, and he was worried about his deer herd? Her mind could barely track the question, much less understand why he'd be asking her. "I suppose," she conceded cautiously.

"Then I can raise all the deer I want right here in Crookston."

A frown tightened her forehead. "What about your ranch?" All those glorious rolling hills he'd described, the wildflowers in spring, the terrible blizzards in winter. The rich, earthy scent of the land he loved.

"I'll sell it and buy something here. Deer are deer, right?"

"But why would you want to sell something you've worked so hard to hold on to? The ranch is your whole life."

It was his turn to frown. Framing her face in his big, strong hands, he said, "You're my life, Hannah Jansen. I love you. If you want me to, I'll be a beet farmer."

Born of tension and excitement, the thrill of love finally acknowledged, a giggle erupted. "Please, not that. I've lived around beet farmers all my life."

"Then what? Name it. I can't ask you to live on a ranch that's so remote you wouldn't have a soul to talk to except a few hired hands. None of 'em very pretty. You'd be bored out of your mind. Besides, you have a business to run."

"Have you got phone lines coming into your place?"

"Sure."

"How 'bout electricity?"

"Yeah, we're on the grid. And when it goes down, which is damn often, particularly in winter, I've got a generator."

She slid her arms up his chest and looped her hands around his neck, her fingers toying with the dark strands of hair at his nape. "Has it occurred to you that any fashion-design business I could run from Minnesota, I could also run from Montana?"

"You could?"

"All I need is my drawing board, a phone, fax so I can order fabric samples, and enough electrical power to run my sewing machine. Plus, now that Jonas has exclusive use of my designs, a few frequent-flyer miles to get me to his offices when he snaps his fingers."

"That's it?" An expression of relief and assertive male confidence spread across Holt's face. "I can give you all that." He dipped his head toward hers with the promise of a kiss.

She planted her palms on his chest. "Wait a minute."

Startled, he backed off. "What's wrong?"

"I'm not easy, you know. I'm not about to go off with any man to the wilds of Montana. Not without certain guarantees."

"What guarantees? I just told you I love you. What more could you ask? We'll get married—"

"Oh?" She cocked her head. "I'd like to be proposed to properly, if it's not too much trouble."

"On my knees?"

"That'd be a good beginning."

"With a ring in hand?"

His grin was suspiciously mischievous. "Tell you what, sweetheart. That gallon of rocky-road ice cream was a special order." He nodded over his shoulder at the bag on the picnic table. "Somewhere in there is a diamond ring that's gonna knock your sweet, sexy teddy off."

Her eyes widened. "Did you bring spoons?"

"Damn right I did. Two of 'em. Big ones."

Laughing, Hannah plowed into the carton of ice cream with gusto. She'd never known chocolate would bring her so much happiness. Nor had she imagined a Montana cowboy would bring her such joy.

Savoring the rich flavor, she looked up into Holt's blue eyes. "Have I mentioned that I love you?"

"I already knew that. Sam Spivak told me. It just took me awhile to believe it was true and realize I love you back."

He did kiss her then, his lips warm, his tongue flavored with a combination of chocolate and an essence that was pure Holt Janson.

Vaguely, in the distance, she heard the alarm sound calling the volunteer firefighters. Mentally, she stifled a groan. She had a terrible feeling another of Marilou's household projects had gone awry.

But for now Hannah cherished the knowledge that she would soon be trading the *e* in her last name for the *o* in Holt's, and that made her a very happy woman.

LOVE & LAUGH

INTO NOVEMBER!

#31 GOING OVERBOARD
Vicki Lewis Thompson

Chance Jefferson was in over his head, stranded on a houseboat with a gorgeous pain in the neck like Andi Lombard. Neither of them knew how to steer the darn thing, and to make matters worse, Chance couldn't keep his hands off his irritating, but oh-so-sexy shipmate. If he fell for Andi, would he sink or swim?

#32 SANDRA AND THE SCOUNDREL
Jacqueline Diamond

Sandra Duval was *not* having a good day. First the mayor snubbed her at a charity fund-raiser! And then she was kidnapped! And swindled out of a fortune. The only way to save the day was to marry her kidnapper. Well, the man was gorgeous and even now Sandra believed you had to look for the silver lining....

Chuckles available now:

#29 ACCIDENTAL ROOMMATES
Charlotte Maclay
#30 WOOING WANDA
Gwen Pemberton

LOVE & LAUGHTER™

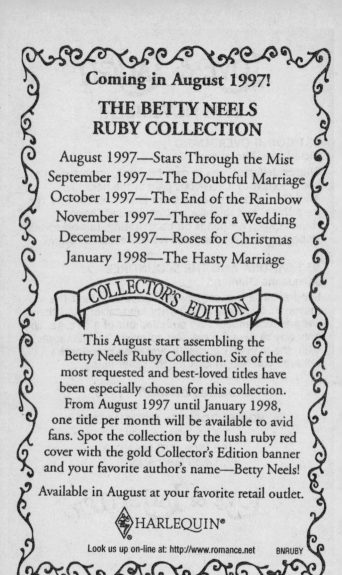

Coming in August 1997!

THE BETTY NEELS RUBY COLLECTION

August 1997—Stars Through the Mist
September 1997—The Doubtful Marriage
October 1997—The End of the Rainbow
November 1997—Three for a Wedding
December 1997—Roses for Christmas
January 1998—The Hasty Marriage

COLLECTOR'S EDITION

This August start assembling the
Betty Neels Ruby Collection. Six of the
most requested and best-loved titles have
been especially chosen for this collection.
From August 1997 until January 1998,
one title per month will be available to avid
fans. Spot the collection by the lush ruby red
cover with the gold Collector's Edition banner
and your favorite author's name—Betty Neels!

Available in August at your favorite retail outlet.

HARLEQUIN®

HARLEQUIN WOMEN KNOW ROMANCE WHEN THEY SEE IT.

And they'll see it on **ROMANCE CLASSICS**, the new 24-hour TV channel devoted to romantic movies and original programs like the special **Harlequin** Showcase of Authors & Stories.

The **Harlequin** Showcase of Authors & Stories introduces you to many of your favorite romance authors in a program developed exclusively for Harlequin readers.

Watch for the **Harlequin** Showcase of Authors & Stories series beginning in the summer of 1997.

If you're not receiving ROMANCE CLASSICS, call your local cable operator or satellite provider and ask for it today!

Escape to the network of your dreams.

ROMANCE CLASSICS

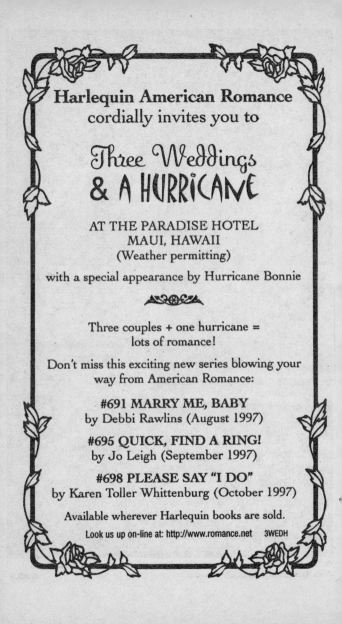

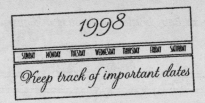

1998

Keep track of important dates

Three beautiful and colorful calendars that celebrate some of the most popular trends in America today.

Look for:

Just Babies—a 16 month calendar that features a full year of absolutely adorable babies!

1998 CALENDAR

Just Babies

16 months of adorable bundles of joy!

Hometown Quilts

1998 Calendar

A 16 month quilting extravaganza!

Hometown Quilts—a 16 month calendar featuring quilted art squares, plus a short history on twelve different quilt patterns.

Inspirations—a 16 month calendar with inspiring pictures and quotations.

Inspirations

A 16 month calendar that will lift your spirits and gladden your heart

Steeple Hill™

♦ HARLEQUIN®

Value priced at $9.99 U.S./$11.99 CAN., these calendars make a perfect gift!

Available in retail outlets in August 1997.   CAL98